Three Circle Star

by

Maggie Shaw

Three Circle Star

by

Maggie Shaw

eregendal.com

First published in the United Kingdom in 2025 by
Eregendal.com, Rosehill Road, Crewe, Cheshire, CW2 8AR.
Printed in the United Kingdom by University of Chester Printers.

ISBN 978-1-7394008-7-3 (paperback)
ISBN 978-1-917389-03-7 (e-book)
ISBN 978-1-917389-04-4 (Kindle version)

Contents

Map of the World
After the Treaty of the Alliance

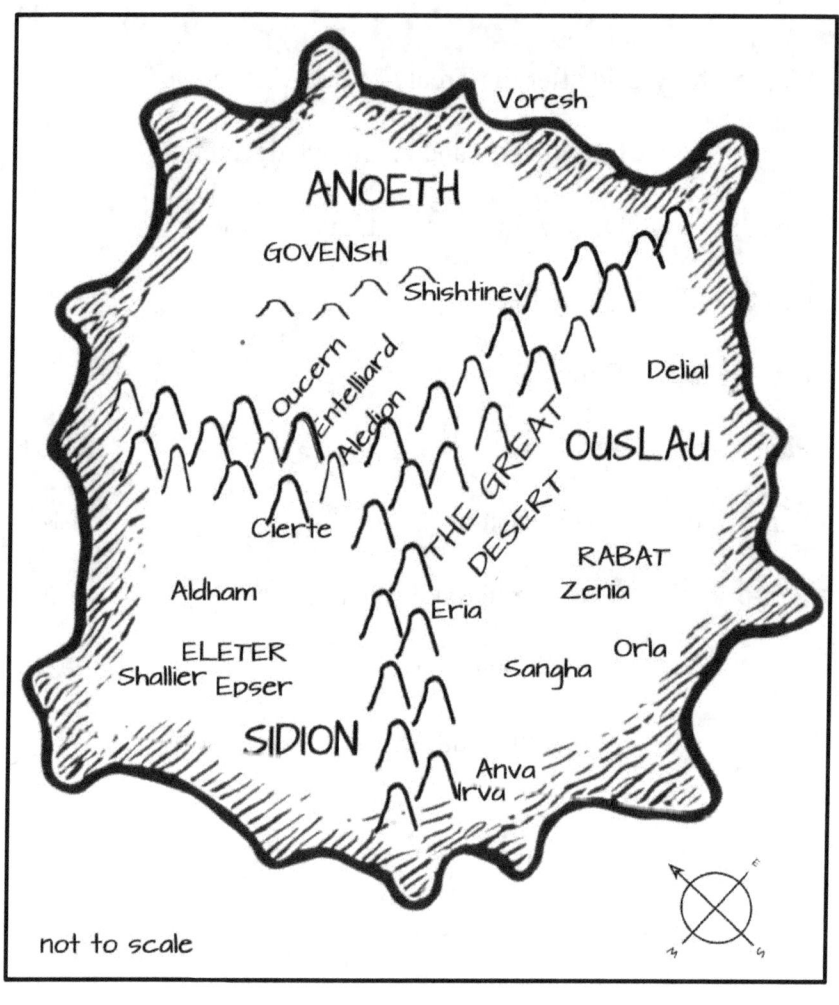

Introduction
and Acknowledgements

Three Circle Star tells the story of a doomed world through the personal stories of three women from different countries who were brought to crisis by the choices they made in life. As Recovery Fiction, it resolves into two different endings, depending on the choices the three women make after they have reached their 'rock bottom'.

The novel was originally written in the late 1970s, but at over 500 pages, it was too long to consider publishing in its original form. It has since undergone extensive editing to tighten up the descriptions and remove some of the world building.

The novel's cryptic title comes from a mythical Doomsday Clock floor in the original story, similar to the tiled floor at the crossing of Chester Cathedral, which shows a star with three haloes. The symbolic three in the story represents the three surviving countries, the three main characters, and the three human divisions of time; past, present and future. The circles relate to all our overlapping and interlocking life stories. The star relates to the name of one of the characters and also the possible fate of the world where the story is set.

As always, I would like to thank those who helped with the book in any way. Special thanks go to those members of Chester Writers who gave me much valuable advice in improving my original manuscript. Any faults in the work are my own alone.

We do not always know whose lives we touch or the difference we make. Each person plays a unique part in humanity's story. So do not give up. The world would be a poorer place without you.

Part 1
Demos the Innkeeper's Story

Welcome to The Travellers Rest at Drysau Bridge. People who enter this inn are lost. Most of them tell me how they came here. I listen, hoping that by letting them tell me their story, I will help them find their way again.

I was lost once, like you. Many years ago, when I was young and foolish, I sought adventure and new horizons. I served under Alcibiades in the naval battle of Notium. His helmsman, Antiochus, sent out a decoy to tempt the Spartans into battle, but the trick backfired and the Spartans defeated us. The injuries I sustained were life-destroying. With my existence hanging in the balance, I found myself here.

The river beneath the bridge flowed with the blood of the martyrs then. It has been dry some sixty years now, but for one shallow pool. The innkeeper gave me a choice: to eat one of the berries growing in the thorns by the river and return to life, or to walk into the sea and let my bones wash up on the shore.

I did not know which to choose. To return to life would mean facing a painful, ignoble existence, but to choose to die was the deed of a coward.

When the innkeeper saw my indecision, he spoke again.

'There is a third alternative, more of a curse than a choice, the one I chose many years ago. Exchange places with me.'

I walked outside into the valley of bones. It stretched far away in every direction from the sea on my right to the misty circle of the distant bordering hills. At my feet lay a human skull. Beyond lay a hundred thousand more. Could all these people have given up and walked into the sea? Could they not have found the courage to eat the berries nourished by the blood of the martyrs? I reflected on the third alternative. Could I escape that choice between the two and instead live here for the rest of my days?

I returned to the inn and offered my hand to the keeper.

'Yes, I agree to take your place,' I said.

We shook hands. On the third shake, he smiled in bliss. His body disintegrated. The dust that had formed him blew away in the breeze.

And here I have been ever since, welcoming lost travellers like you, and listening to your stories.

Now I have told you my tale, I shall set out three places at the table for you. While we eat, it would be good to hear how each of you came here. Who will begin?

Part 2
Ginny Lee's Story

2:1

My problems all started with a spiked drink. I didn't know it at the time, but it nearly wrecked my career.

I came round, sitting on a bench in the rain. A giant poster next to me was perpetuating the mother myth with a twelve-foot-high image of a white-haired old lady. Her plump face smiled as she held a brightly wrapped present in her hands, half opened to reveal a box of Wiener's chocolates. Above her gleamed the words, *Happy Mother's Day, Mum.*

In my lap lay a box of Wiener's chocolates and a greetings card covered in psychedelic flowers. I wondered why I had bought Mother the present when I needed the money to pay the fare to Kitty Derrer's. Then I tried to remember why I wanted to see Kitty Derrer. I looked through my wet pockets and found a crumpled photo of her. The round face and long black hair looked familiar. She had written on the back of the photo, *Meet me when the Moon is full in Shallier.* Yes, I remembered: I had promised to see her there. But that must have been three months ago, before New Year.

I looked up at the moon. It was struggling to shine through the rain clouds, but it looked big and fat and round. Was I already too late to see her?

A bright blue bus slowed down at the junction. The windows were filled with posters of smiling people travelling to South Kenham, the area of Eleter where Mother lived. I hopped on the back of the bus and hopped off again just before the ticket clippie reached me to ask for the fare.

I alighted on a busy street. People pushed past me, faceless with waxen masks. They wielded black umbrellas in their left hands and heavy brown briefcases in their right. They were the army of clerical workers who commuted every day between the little boxes they called home in suburbia and their offices. I looked for my father in their ranks, because he was a sergeant in the army of office workers. But he too wore a waxen mask all the time he was away from home, so I wouldn't recognise him even if I saw him in the crowd.

Mother's fashionable *pied-à-terre* luxury apartment was on the second floor of a terraced villa in a prestigious street. The *pied-à-terre* style was all the rage at that time, as if only yesterday's people lived in houses they didn't have to share. As I walked up the steps to the front door, a car drew over to the kerb and two women alighted.

I rang the bell and huddled in a corner of the porch to give the women room to shelter from the rain. Their sweet spicy perfume beguiled my senses. Cracked clown masks hid their faces, with bright red cheeks and lips, bright green eye shadow and white foreheads. Though their blonde wigs were permed upwards to give the illusion of height, they were easily six inches shorter than me. The bodices of their long white dresses were bedecked with paste jewels. The fleshy hands clasping their bleached fun-fur rabbit stoles gleamed with fake gem rings. Bejewelled chokers held up their sagging chins.

'Who is it?' Mother asked through the intercom.

'Conny and Asha,' said the two women, giggling.

The latch buzzed and the front door opened. I followed the women up two flights of stairs to Mother's front door. Mother was waiting for them on the landing. She was six inches shorter than me, with a blonde wig piled up to make her look taller. Her long white halter-neck dress glittered with diamante and her hands, ears and neck sparkled with paste gems. Her face was hidden behind a waxy, clownish mask.

She flung her arms round the two women in welcome and turned to lead them in, not having seen me.

'Mother,' I said.

She turned to look at me with blank eyes. I touched her hand. Her pupils cleared and she looked up brightly into my face.

'Ginny! I'm so glad you could come.'

'I've brought you a present. For Mother's Day.'

I offered her the wet box of chocolates and card. She took them without looking at them and set them aside on a whatnot shelf as she ushered me into the lounge.

'I wish you wouldn't dress so sombrely, Ginny. Denim and black are so dull. Why don't you wear bright colours like ours?'

'Yes, white is bright, Mother,' I said.

I looked to see if I could recognise Conny and Asha in the crowd of guests wearing blonde wigs and long white halter-neck dresses, but they had disappeared in the sea of masked faces. Mother was the only person I could recognise, as she had pinned a silk orchid on her bosom.

'Do you want something to eat, Ginny? You look very hungry.'

I let her guide me to the table of party food. She carved off a leg from a cold roast fowl and arranged it on a plate with a salad. I took it from her with my left hand. A guest placed a glass of whiskey in my right hand. We must have met before sometime, as she knew my favourite drink. Mother's guests surrounded us, all women. They clucked in admiration at how different Mother and I looked.

I sipped my whiskey. It tasted like water, as Mother's drink always did. I took a second sip to make sure. It still tasted like water. I placed my glass on the table and heard it groan in protest. With a hand free, I risked a bite from the chicken leg. It tasted like cardboard, as Mother's food always did. I took a second bite. It still tasted of cardboard. I longed to swap the plate of chicken salad for some processed food, something I could taste.

'Mother, do you have any baked beans?' I asked.

'You're not still eating out of tins, are you?' she complained. 'I thought you had a good job. Daddy says it's a good job. That's why he got it for you.'

'Now is not the time, Mother. Let's wait until I get back,' I said, trying to avoid the scene that always followed my requests for tinned food.

'I cannot wait until you get back!'

Her higher voice warned me her mask was cracking. I quickly guided her through the throng of guests into the quiet of her study before she embarrassed herself in front of them. She switched on the desk lamp as I closed the door.

'What has been happening to you lately, Ginny?' she demanded. Her gaudy smile had dribbled red streaks down her chin.

'It's been raining for three months, Mother.'

She sighed and looked away. 'Oh, something's triggered you again!' Her mask dropped an inch as she looked back at me. 'Why haven't you been to see Mr Sinclair recently? I pay him a lot of money for you to talk with him whenever you want.'

'You can't buy friends. I couldn't talk to Mr Sinclair if my life depended on it. He doesn't even believe in real dictionaries.'

'Real dictionaries? Of course he doesn't! You haven't been seeing Benson again, have you?'

'What if I have?'

'He's pulling you downhill, Ginny. All that nonsense about real dictionaries is destroying your ability to reason.'

'They're not nonsense! Or are you saying that *giant* doesn't mean *small*, and *new and improved* doesn't mean *smaller for the same price?*'

'Ginny! I despair of you!'

Mother's broken mask fell from her face and lay melting by the lamp on the desktop. Her real face looked so much more beautiful than the clown mask that had dropped.

'I'm sorry, Mother. I didn't mean to hurt you.'

I put my arms around her waist to comfort her and realised how thin she was under the padding of her long white dress. Why did she go to such lengths to keep in with her crowd of false friends?

'Mother, I need your help. I have to go and see Kitty Derrer. She lives in Shallier, and I haven't got the fare. It's important I go tonight, because she's superstitious, so she wants me to come when there's a full moon. The moon looks pretty full already. I don't want to miss it and be forced to wait another month in grotty Paddingham.'

'O my precious! You do end up with such strange friends. Do you have a photo of her?'

I pulled out the damp, crumpled photo and let her look at Kitty's round face and long black hair.

'Oh, isn't she lovely! Of course I can help you.' Mother found some keys in a drawer of the desk and placed them by the light. 'Look, I haven't any money in the apartment, but if you go and see Daddy, he'll give you some. You can take my car to get there. Make sure you bring it back in three days though – I will need it that morning.'

'Thanks, Mother. And don't worry. I'll be back in two days at the latest.'

I pocketed the keys and escaped to the safety of the door. As I opened it, I looked back. She was punching out a number on her phone. Her clown mask covered her face again, intact once more as she returned to the falseness of her glittering social whirl. The false front glistened eerily in the low light.

'Just phoning Daddy for you,' she said.

'Thanks, Mother. Have a good Mother's Day, whenever it is.'

'I will. Safe journey. Do try the spicy chicken on your way out. You should find it more to your liking than the salad.'

The party guests gathered round me as I emerged from the study.

'Aren't you a handsome young thing,' they said, complimenting me to my face but, I knew from the past, they criticised me behind my back. I picked up the bowl of spicy chicken from the party fare and took it out onto the balcony to eat in peace.

The rain was teeming down in the street, but I stayed relatively dry on the balcony, as the wall of the building sheltered me from the wind. The double-glazed balcony doors muted the babble of the party guests behind me. For a moment, I felt peace.

A taxi drew up and Sinclair got out. I swore! Mother had betrayed me, yet again! I should have known the gift of the car keys hid something devious. Her gifts always did. She hadn't expected me to be free to drive away.

It was pointless trying to leave by the apartment door, as Sinclair would come up that way. I used instead the route I had used many times before.

Next door's balcony was only three feet away, across a two-storey drop. I climbed up onto the stone parapet, turned to face the wall and used it to support me as my left leg swung out to find the neighbouring parapet. When I had a firm foothold, I moved my weight onto the neighbours' parapet and dropped down onto their balcony.

As usual, the Messengers' balcony doors were unlocked – they did not expect burglars to climb that high. I dived inside, closed the curtains and waited a couple of minutes to make sure Sinclair had cleared the stairs.

'Mummy,' a child called softly, sobbing.

I froze briefly, fearing a trap.

'Is that you, Mummy?' the child called.

The voice opened a door into my past. It wrung my emotions with my grief for all the times I had been left alone in the house while my father worked and Mother partied with her girlfriends, in those lonely years before they finally admitted defeat and got divorced. I followed the sound of the voice into a box-room sized bedroom, with the name *Dawn* on the door.

A girl of about six or seven lay weeping in bed, her red face and damp hair visible in a low night light. I knelt down beside her.

'Don't cry, Dawn. I'm Ginny Lee. Your mummy asked me to keep an eye on you.'

'I know you, Ginny. I've seen you next door. When will Mummy be back?'

'Not long, Dawn, not long. Would you like me to sing you to sleep? Then when you wake up, she'll be here again.'

She nodded, just a slight movement of the head. Encouraged, I sang her a lullaby I had learned at school. As I sang, a part of me wished I could take her away and be a proper mother to her, unlike her own mother and my mother. But I had nothing else to offer her than understanding.

Dawn's eyelids drifted shut. Soon, her regular breathing told me she was asleep. I crept out of the apartment so as not to wake her and made my escape.

2:2

I returned to my rather less fashionable *pied-à-terre* bedsit in Paddingham before going to visit my father, because I needed to find out what had happened in the last three months. The room was on the top floor of a crumbling four-storey terraced house on the main road. The woodwork needed a coat of paint, the hall carpets were threadbare and the light bulbs dim. All was covered in the amber patina of grime.

My room was on the front of the house, a nine-foot by ten-foot box with a bed, a cooker, a wardrobe, a threadbare armchair, a cupboard and a kitchen sink. The traffic noise was constant. I checked for food in the cupboard but it was so mouldy, I threw it out. My journal lay on the shelf below. I opened it and started reading, hoping to find some clues.

Most of the entries had been written in a kind of code I could no longer fathom. The ones that weren't banged on incoherently about truth and light. So I must have been on another bender.

My neighbour Benson knocked at my door, asking in his reedy voice if I was OK. I hid the journal away in the cupboard and let him in. He settled in the chair, forcing me to sit cross-legged on the bed.

'What's been happening these past three months, Ben?'

'I dunno, Gin. You seemed out of it most of the time. A really bad trip. We didn't see much of you at all. And when we did, you kept saying it was raining when it wasn't. You were really gone! By the way, Marcus has

17

asked me to say he's sorry.'

'About what?'

Benson became evasive. It told me he knew but did not want to be disloyal to his partner. His left hand was covering the tear in his jeans from his last arrest for possession. The guy he got done with had died in the police cells. He couldn't forget.

'You kept telling me you couldn't read anything, Gin: you could only read things that were true, and everything in print was a lie. So I told you about my "real" dictionaries. You were a bit obsessive about those.'

Things started to fall into place for me. I had always had an issue about people with false fronts who never told the truth. Like all the masked women at Mother's party, and so often Mother herself.

'Did I talk about masks at all?'

His eyes rolled. 'Oh, yes! All the time. You said I was the only one who doesn't have one.'

'Ben, the last thing I remember before today was being in your flat on New Year's Eve. What happened at your party?'

His eyes dropped, and he became evasive again. 'I don't know, Gin. I was out of it. Just Marcus says he's sorry. He didn't think it would hit you like it did.'

'What, Benson?'

'You'll have to ask him. I gotta go.'

And go he did. He escaped into the hall and thudded down the stairs. Instead of stopping on the first floor to return to his flat, he carried on down to the ground floor and left by the front door.

I was furious with Marcus. He had never liked me, ever since he and Benson had become an item. He thought I would steal Benson from him, not understanding that Benson and I only ever saw each other as friends. Part of me wanted to go down and bang on his door and shout a few obscenities. But I resisted the urge. Now that I had some idea of what happened, it was time to visit my father.

2:3

The night journey down to Ewlham in Mother's two-seater sports car was stormy. The wheels splashed, the engine roared, the wipers swished and thunder cracked. Behind these, an orchestral suite played to the tempest. Backed by a continuo of strings, a mournful flute leapt from its heights to my depths, bidding me follow it towards the dawn. Over this, Kitty Derrer sang a distant song with no meaning which stabbed through my heart.

I slammed my foot on the brake. The car skidded to a halt just a few inches from a van at the end of a queue of traffic. A red sign beside me warned *Heavy Plant Crossing*. When the traffic had not moved in five minutes, I got out of the car and strolled along the queued vehicles to a knot of drivers at the head. Across the road lay a large tree trunk. Lights blazed on the tree to help the workmen see to put chains around it.

Panic surged up in me. The juxtaposition of the *Heavy Plant Crossing* sign and the shifting tree took me into a parallel world where trees crossed roads as well as deer. I fought to resist the tempting hallucination and its route back into oblivion. My hands shook and my face sweated with the effort and the start of withdrawal symptoms. Desperate to appear normal, I stuffed my hands in my pockets and edged closer to hear what the workmen were saying.

'A lightning strike. Lucky no one was caught by the tree as it fell,' one said.

'How long will it take to clear?' asked a driver.

'A couple of hours. Your best bet is to take a detour through the housing estate.'

'Where's that?' the driver asked.

He could not have been from around there, as everyone local knew the route. Its warren of avenues would make a great place to dodge someone if you thought they were following you.

'A turning a quarter of a mile back,' I said. 'You can do a big loop and rejoin the road just outside Ewlham. If you're not sure, follow my sports car.'

So, I ended up leading a convoy of cars, vans and a couple of trucks through one of the most exclusive residential areas in that part of the suburbs. Halfway through, we met a convoy of similar vehicles coming from the other direction.

The residents must have felt pretty cross with us that night. Their white-walled houses with red-tiled roofs lined our route. I knew what was beyond their front walls: family upon family of faceless father, masked mother, bullying older son and screaming younger daughter. They gathered round their screens watching the advertisers' fiction that made father feel insignificant, mother inadequate, son cheated and daughter jealous. Meanwhile, in far off Aldham, granny upon granny sat, like my own, in a house with no heating, hoping the family would call her, holding back her tears and praying they would not sign her into a healthtel. But they were too busy letting the ad writers make them feel dissatisfied.

So it was late when I drew up outside my father's detached white house with its red-tiled roof. I parked on his semicircular drive. For a moment, I watched the rain gleam as it passed through the shaft of light escaping through a chink in the living room curtains. Once I had built up my courage, I ran from the car into the porch and rang the doorbell.

Inside, a blaring television was quickly silenced. My father opened the front door. He looked like a dummy from Ailson's The Tailor's shop window. He had a waxy face, false black hair with false grey streaks and false sideburns. His dark-blue trousers were modestly flared in the latest style, matching his dark-blue tie and contrasting with his orange shirt. He looked exactly like the middle-aged conformist he was, trying to dress in the style of a non-existent younger set. Only his socks made a personal statement: they were a subtle khaki.

'Ginny! Come in, come in out of this dreadful rain. How are you, my dear? Haven't seen you for weeks!'

'Sorry I'm so late, Father. A tree had blocked the road. I had to come the long way round.'

He ushered me in and sat me down in his lounge, in an armchair by the giant grey television screen. I watched him as he fussed around, getting me a glass of whiskey and a cigarette and a bowl of crisps and a plate of biscuits, to show his 'hospitality'. Then he sat with some crisps in one hand, a whiskey in the other, a cigarette burning in an ashtray and a nibbled biscuit on the arm of his chair, to show that his 'hospitality' was no bother because he had wanted to eat, drink and smoke all at once, but had been too interested in a TV programme to bother; until his guest had arrived who was so much more interesting than the silly TV documentary about a social problem in Paddingham.

'So, what have you been up to recently, Ginny?'

Something in his tone warned me from past experience that the visit was about to get frosty. I needed to keep on his sweet side to get the money to go to Shallier and see Kitty Derrer.

'I've been doing some research. Into truth and light.'

'Virginia, you were meant to be in Shallier three months ago. Why didn't you go?'

It was another light-bulb moment for me. My father knew about my going to meet Kitty Derrer.

'I was waiting for the full moon.'

'What kind of superstitious claptrap is that? And even if it were true, which it isn't, we've already had two full moons since you agreed to go.'

My head dropped. I pulled out Kitty's photograph with trembling hands and showed him the message on the back. He took one look, sighed and lowered his shaking head. When he looked back up, his expression was resigned.

'Why do you take everything so literally? You were just meant to meet her in the pub, after 9 pm, the week after New Year. You've been on another bender, haven't you?'

'I didn't do it deliberately, Father. One moment, I'm at a New Year's Eve party, the next moment, I'm sitting on a bench holding a Mother's Day present.'

'You've really fried your brain this time, haven't you! You could have ruined everything! Let's just hope you've left no evidence for once.'

'Will you help me get to Shallier, then? I've got Mother's car. I only need fuel.'

'Yes, I will help you get there. But you can't go now – it's too late, and I can see you've got the shakes again. Stop here overnight. You'll need to leave first thing tomorrow and stop off somewhere to kill time – we can't have you going straight to Shallier from here in case it comes back on me.'

'But that shouldn't matter.'

'Virginia, don't you remember anything from your studies? I'm a civil servant. Whatever my beliefs, I must have nothing to do with politics.'

More memories flocked back to me: earning my political degree at uni, Father's frustration with our present government, our political debates when I was younger about fairness for all and the appalling damage done in the pursuit of profit and wealth.

He went on, 'As I clearly can't trust you with any money, I'll phone the garage in the morning to give you some credit for fuel. Our issue now is, can we trust you at all?'

2:4

True to his word, Father arranged for his local garage to fill my car with fuel first thing next morning. I set off for Shallier with a sandwich and a flask of tea from Father's kitchen, but I couldn't meet Kitty until the evening. How could I spend a day without being spotted? Most of it, I lay low in a library in a town some thirty miles off the quickest route there. When the library closed, I visited a nearby gallery which was open late that evening, displaying a curious collection of amateur creativity, from paintings and pottery to petit point and pin cushions.

I arrived at The Moon in Shallier about an hour before closing time. The pub had the look of a collection of wings added on to a small inn wherever the narrow Shallier roads allowed. Its walls were painted white to hide the additions,. Someone with a sense of humour had painted its pub sign, depicting a realistic satellite being nibbled by mice against a starry sky. Expensive cars filled the few parking spaces, and the establishment exuded an air of opulence. It was not a place I would normally frequent.

Would Kitty even be in the pub when I was three months late, I wondered. I put on my brave face to enter. The crowded place was hot and noisy. A wall of people hampered my attempts to search for her in the many bars. The Moon was certainly full that night.

After some time pushing through the crowd, I found Kitty in a small upstairs room called The Study. She was sitting with a couple of men at a table for six. A cocktail and two beers stood in front of them. No one else was using the room.

Kitty looked radiant. Her long, bushy black hair framed her heart-shaped face. A batik ethnic dress flattered her shapely upper body.

'Ginny! You've finally made it!' she called out, waving. 'Come and sit with us. I want you to meet my husband, Sam, and our friend Dulane Ellis.'

I shook hands with the men and sat at their table. Her husband looked like a civil servant, but his vigorous handshake crushed my fingers. Dulane looked lean in their well-fed company. He had a narrow face and intense eyes which seemed to see through me. His gentle handhold lingered longer than I expected.

'I'm sorry it's taken me so long to get here. A couple of neighbours delayed me,' I said.

They looked at each other.

'We know, Ginny,' Kitty said. 'Your adventures over the last few months have established you firmly as a resident of Paddingham and a local "character". When we first asked you to make yourself known in the area, we didn't intend quite that much exposure.'

'Not that that's a problem,' Dulane said. 'We fixed things so that none of your escapades turned out to your detriment. But we'll need to make sure you tone things down from now on.'

I looked into his eyes and melted. I would have promised him anything. Unable to speak for lust, I just nodded.

'We checked out Benson's boyfriend, Marcus, after you went haywire,' said Sam. 'Turns out he was nobbled by the Commercialist party. They got him to set you up so their election candidate would have no real opposition. Have nothing more to do with him.'

I shook my head. It was a struggle to say, 'But he lives in the same house.'

'Not for long,' said Sam, with a look that warned me he could be dangerous.

'Are you still willing to go ahead?' Kitty asked.

'If you are, we need you to sign on the dotted line,' Dulane said.

He passed a document to me. It was a work contract. The job was to stand as an independent candidate in the next general election, contesting the Paddingham constituency. Some financial backing had been secured, but I would be expected to raise funds to support my campaign and pay my wages.

'So you want me to be the gullible fool who fronts The Network at the next election?'

'We want you to be you. Ginny: the fiery campaigner with a heart for the poor and the marginalised,' Kitty said. 'The people we're trying to reach would spot a fake a mile off.'

It was my dream job! My training, my politics, the way I thought about life. I could hardly believe something so wonderful was being offered me on a plate. There had to be a catch.

'What happened to the funding?' I asked. 'Didn't you tell me once you had it all set up?'

'Our anonymous second backer turned out to be Roul Khoury, so we had to say no,' Sam said. 'We've got to get in first, before we risk being backed by people like him.'

I took little persuading.

'Yes, I do want to do this. Where do I sign?'

Dulane turned the document to the back page. I signed it with a flourish where he indicated. Sam and Kitty countersigned.

They then gave me a second document, a completed application form for me to stand in the election, which Dulane countersigned as my election agent. With my signature on that form, the trajectory of my life changed direction for good.

2:5

I drove back to the capital next morning to return Mother's sports car. Dulane followed me in his black saloon. From there, he took me to Government House to lodge the election candidacy form.

Lodging the form was our first challenge. As I only rented a *pied-à-terre* bedsit in Paddingham and paid for my utilities by coin meter, I had no bills to confirm my identity. My driving licence on its own was not enough.

'This is the sort of problem that stops young people registering to vote,' I told Dulane. 'The dice are loaded against them from the start.'

'We'll find a way, Ginny,' he replied with that whimsical smile that made me melt.

He drove me over to my place and followed me up the stairs to my battered bedsit door. Standing by the door on the hinge side was a carton of long life milk. I picked it up as I always did and took it inside.

'Did you order that, Ginny?'

'I must have done, though I don't remember doing so.'

'Don't touch it!'

I looked back at him, shocked by his harsh tone.

'Why not?'

'Let's send it away to get tested first. We wondered how they kept you drugged up. This may have been the way they did it.'

He wrapped the carton in a plastic bag, while I dug out a recent Student Loan statement.

On our return trip to Government House, the official accepted the statement as my proof of identity and let us lodge the form. Dulane paid the large deposit out of his own bank account. We got back in the black saloon car, waving the receipt in joy at our success.

Our next task was to set up a campaign office in Paddingham. Dulane wanted to ask the council to provide us with one. I told him we should look at the high street first.

Paddingham High Street was on its last legs. Most of the shops were boarded up, and the windows were rotting and caked with grime. The only places still open were betting shops, off licences and corner shop food stores. Dulane tried to hide his distaste, but it showed in his pursed lips and squinting eyes.

'Welcome to the real Paddingham, Dulane. It's the cheapest place to live in town, but when you move here, your only way is down.'

The rental sign boards over the vacant shops gave us some contact numbers. The first place we contacted was an estate agent whose name Dulane recognised. When we explained what we needed the office for and our limited budget, the agent's tone changed.

'We only have this property available,' he said, and told us about an old bike shop on the edge of the area we wanted. 'Two hundred a week, with utilities and service charges on top.'

'But that's five times the going rate for property in that area!' Dulane protested.

'They don't want to rent to us, Dulane. Let's move on!'

The next number connected us to a housing association. A woman with a tired voice answered our call. She offered us the run-down shop we were interested in for 200 per month, about the going rate. I thanked her and said we would be in touch if we wanted to make an application.

'But we might lose the property if we don't snap it up,' Dulane protested as I closed the call.

'That shop's been empty for months. There's not going to be a sudden rush for it this afternoon,' I said. 'Now let's go to the grocery store.'

'We want to get a shop, not shopping!'

'You'll see.'

I knew the proprietor, Nahal Singh, well as I often shopped for food in his store. It stood halfway up High Street and was flanked by two empty shops, which he also owned. He smiled as we came in.

'It's good to see you, Miss Ginny. You're looking a lot better today.'

'I've got a new job, Mr Singh. I've come to ask you for some help.'

'Now, you know I don't give credit.'

'It's nothing like that. I've been chosen to fight the election for the Paddingham seat on an independent socialist ticket. I need a High Street address for my campaign headquarters. Would you be willing to rent us the shop next door?'

'You are a brave girl, but you are going to lose. None of the people who would vote for you can register. The people who are registered, wouldn't want to vote for you. They've done very well out of our present Representative.'

'I have a plan to deal with that. That's why I need a place on Paddingham High Street – a place where people can come and get help to register and other things.'

His face changed. A faint ray of hope lifted his tired, fatalistic expression.

'I like the idea of that, Miss Ginny. People often ask me for help, but what do I know? I used to send them to the library, but that's gone too, now. If you opened such a place, I could send them to you instead.'

'How much would you charge us for rent?'

He shook his head. 'You've no money, Miss Ginny. I can't see you getting elected and I don't want to put you in debt. So I wouldn't charge you. Just do the place up for me instead.'

'Oh, but we will get in!'

He beamed. 'All right. As you are so confident, I will let you have the shop next door at number 29 rent free until you get elected into office. In return, you will do the place up for me. There is a lot of rubbish to throw out after the last tenants, and you'll need to paint and decorate and fix the windows and clean. If you are elected, we will draw up a new contract to include rent. Do you agree?'

Of course I agreed. Mr Singh promised to get a proper contract drawn up for us to sign. Then he let us into the property to measure up and clear the place a bit.

It had been a charity shop and unusable donations lay scattered across the floors in every room, downstairs and up. After our inspection, Dulane stood in the shop window and shook his head in disbelief.

'How did you manage that, Ginny?'

'I know Mr Singh. He is a good man. He believes in community. I've seen him help a mother who couldn't feed her child and a confused old man who couldn't remember who he was. I was expecting him to ask us for a very low rent. Instead, all we need is some paint and a lot of effort.'

'I'm sure we'll be able to call on some of our Network friends to help with that.'

'The Network? But I thought we weren't taking donations from Roul Khoury.'

'Not financial ones – we have to report those, and they can be traced back to the donor. But willing volunteers are OK.'

Before the ink had dried on the contract, our first volunteers came over to clean, repair, paint and take the rubbish away. Two weeks later, the dowdy shop at 29 gleamed with fresh white paintwork and brick red lettering on the signboard. Some used office furniture was delivered the week after that, and we held our grand opening on the first of the month. Our election campaign could finally begin.

2:6

Dulane proved to be a very good publicist. We had settled on The Drop In Centre as the name for number 29, with the subtitle 'Ginny Lee's Constituency Office' in smaller letters below to make it clear it was a political establishment. The opening of The Drop In appeared in all the local media, and a crowd gathered there to enjoy our free food and non-alcoholic drinks at the launch party.

Dulane insisted I consumed only food and drink I had bought myself after he read the analysis report for the carton of milk he had found on my doorstep. The milk had contained a cocktail of illegal drugs, in a combination that could easily cause a three month black out. I must have come out of it by chance by not returning to my bedsit for several days. Looking back on the episode, I realised I should have recognised it as a drug spike with the constant rain and everyone in masks. But that would have required coherent thinking which I didn't have at the time.

Shortly after we received the report, Marcus disappeared. Benson told me he had been beaten up one night as they were leaving a dive. I recalled Sam Derrer's manner and was not surprised. Benson spent some weeks in the same sort of oblivion as I had done. When he finally came to, he spent all his time at The Drop In, making hot drinks and doing the washing up. It was all he was capable of doing for some time.

He was a great help to us. We were inundated with people wanting help, guidance and advice. The opening rush of the first week did not slacken off at all. So many needy people called on us, we recruited and trained volunteer support workers from The Network to cope with them all. I suspected Roul Khoury paid the volunteers behind our backs: how else could they have afforded to live in the capital while working with us each day? Dulane told me to ask no questions there.

After a month of problem-solving for our constituents, and others from further afield, we moved into the next phase of our campaign. A business called The Training Bureau let us have some administration trainees as interns to create election leaflets and deliver them to every address in the constituency. The leaflets included simple instructions on how to register to vote in the forthcoming election, with an invitation to come to The Drop In if there were any problems registering.

That brought in droves more people needing help. It seemed as if the system had been stacked against them. For Dulane, this was another PR opportunity. We held a rally in the local park one sunny day, during which I made a speech of protest about the way the authorities were deliberately disenfranchising those at the bottom of the social scale. My photo flooded the local media yet again. Feeling the criticism, my political rivals began to fight back.

The other Paddingham election candidates started drop-in sessions at their constituency offices. They put out press statements discrediting me for being a drunk and a drug addict with no political experience. The national media got hold of the story and ran with it, printing derogatory photos of me during my weeks-long black out that had been provided by my rival candidates. The Derrers had not managed to suppress everything, after all.

I was in tears as I showed Dulane the newspaper version of the story. He laughed and patted my hand.

'Don't worry, Ginny. Any publicity for us is good publicity. You're not just a local phenomenon now, you're a national one! We'll counter this rubbish with a story showing all the good you're doing here, the good you've had to come and do after years of political neglect by the other parties. Then in a few days, we'll tell the tale of your amazing recovery after your rivals' plot to stop you through spiking your milk with a cocktail of drugs.'

I nodded to show I understood him, but I still sobbed.

'I need to take some time out, Dulane. It's all getting a bit too much.'

'Of course. Go out the back. Don't let the bastards see they've made you cry, or they'll come for you even more.'

The back was a courtyard we shared with Nahal Singh's grocery store and the empty shop on his other side. I sat on a broken chair and wept. After a few minutes, Nahal Singh joined me. He offered me some spicy chai in a white utility mug. My hands shook as I held it.

I apologised to him for crying. 'It's all just got on top of me. I work so hard for these people, and then they stab me in the back in the papers.'

He drew up another broken chair and sat beside me in the morning sunshine.

'They are not the same people, Miss Ginny.' He paused briefly. 'There are also many people who are very proud of you. It is a great privilege for me to tell others I know you. I am so happy that you are using my empty shop to do such good. These people who come to you had no place to turn to before. Please don't let them down.'

'I don't want to, but the weight is so heavy.'

'I know. I will tell Mr Dulane you must have a week's holiday. Somewhere with no pressures: just trees and waters and hills and green fields.'

'But what would I do?'

He smiled. 'Read a book? Go for a walk? Talk about the weather. Ignore the news.'

Dulane came outside, looking displeased.

'Ah, there you are, Ginny. You're needed in the call centre. Two of the girls are late going to their lunch.'

I leapt up to obey. Mr Singh caught my arm to hold me back.

'Mr Dulane, Miss Ginny needs a break, too. Let the callers wait a little longer.'

'There will be time enough for breaks after the election!'

I put down my mug of tea and turned for the door.

'Miss Ginny, take your drink with you. And Mr Dulane, do not kill the goose that lays the golden eggs.'

2:7

A fortnight later, I was walking from my house to The Drop In, when a large black car with dark windows screeched to a halt beside me. Two men in black leapt out and pulled me onto the back seat, one gripping my mouth with a hand. The car raced off into the morning traffic. I struggled against their hold but only made them grip more fiercely.

'Don't make a fuss, and you'll be all right,' ordered the man on my right, his fingers digging into my right arm. I looked at his face but only saw two eyes. Like his two partners in crime, he wore a black ski mask over his face. I felt the point of a six-inch knife press against my ribs.

Too petrified to speak, I nodded to show I understood. The man released my mouth.

'Who put you up to this?' I asked, sounding braver than I felt.

'You'll see soon enough.'

Different outcomes flashed through my mind, each worse than the last. I reined in such thoughts: only a clear head would let me spot some weakness and escape. It wasn't the first time I had faced knives and I had survived them, so I would come through this too.

The car escaped the rush-hour traffic by turning down some rat runs and came out along a service road less than a mile from the snatch. One side of the road was bordered by railway arches. The driver turned under one of these and stopped beside a small grey car.

The men transferred me to the other car and drove off at a normal speed. Just one man sat beside me in the back seat. He still pressed his knife against my ribs.

'Where are you taking me?' I asked, my heart pounding.

'You'll see soon enough,' he repeated.

Half an hour later, the car turned into a semi-derelict area of disused warehouses and came to a halt by the loading bay of an old flour mill. We had barely stopped when a team of six armed officers leapt out of the shadows, their assault rifles aimed at the men in the car.

'Throw out your weapons!' shouted an officer.

My captors hesitated.

'I said, throw out your weapons!' he repeated, louder and more urgently.

The kidnappers wound down the car windows and tossed out their guns and the knife. What a relief not to have the blade against my ribs! But my heart was still pounding as I faced this new confrontation.

An officer moved warily towards the car and kicked the weapons away. Then he backed off again.

'Now get out the car, with your hands up!'

The three kidnappers looked at each other before swinging their doors open and stepping out onto the concrete yard. My door wouldn't open. I had to slide across the back seat to get out the other side.

'Ginny Lee! Walk away from the car towards the door. Slowly!'

I obeyed, praying that the kidnappers weren't carrying other arms. The twenty feet to the door took an eternity. As I neared it, a female officer pulled me into the doorway to shelter me. We pressed against the rotting wood, out of the line of fire, while her colleagues dealt with the kidnappers. I guessed what happened next from the noises they made.

The officers threw the three kidnappers against their car, handcuffed them, checked them for weapons, and bundled them into a waiting vehicle.

'All clear. You can come out now!' one called.

I stumbled out of the doorway with the female officer's support.

'Are you OK?' she asked me.

My brave front cracked at this first slight hint of sympathy, and I wept. Again, I wept! Me, who was always so strong, who could cope with anything! Maybe could cope with anything as long as I had a slug of rotgut or a line or two inside.

I shook my head and let her take me away to another car. We sat in the back seat, but this time there was no knife pressing into me. She was dressed like her colleagues in a uniform I didn't recognise, very dark-blue fatigues with a matching patrol cap. Her face looked hard, like she had seen many things in action and didn't think much of them. In other circumstances, I would not have trusted her.

The car took us to an anonymous office block on the edge of the city centre. There she took me to a windowless interview room, where she and her colleague questioned me about the kidnapping. They were persistent interrogators, repeating the same questions in different ways to see if they could trip me up.

Eventually, they seemed satisfied and ended the interview. As they left the room, a familiar voice greeted me from the open door.

'Ginny?'

I leapt to my feet in joy and relief.

'Dad!' I cried.

I ran into his arms and clutched him. He hugged me with such affection I wanted to cry. After a few moments, he gently prised me off and led me out of the room, reassuring me that once we were on our way, we could talk. An officer escorted us out of the building. Soon we were in Father's car heading out of town up the North Road.

'I'm so glad you're safe, Ginny. I don't know what I would have done if something had happened to you.'

'Father, I thought you'd given up on me. I haven't seen you since that awful night just before Mother's Day.'

'No, I have never given up on you. Your mother and I have watched your campaign from the sidelines, and we're proud of what you are achieving.'

'Did your work stop you from contacting me, Father?'

'You called me Dad just now. I liked that. Do use it again if you feel able. No, it wasn't my department. Your election agent, Dulane, has been a bit too protective.'

'He's the one who's made it all happen, Dad. He's so special. I owe him so much.'

'You don't owe him your health. Mr Singh phoned me. He said you need a holiday. He fears you may crack under the pressure.'

'Mr Singh? Since when did he have your phone number?'

'Since the beginning of the year, after you didn't turn up at Shallier. Now, don't pout. He's not a snitch. I asked about you at his shop. He was very helpful, so I gave him my card and asked him to let me know if you were in real trouble.'

'So was he the one who arranged for me to be kidnapped in broad daylight? I was petrified!'

'No, that wasn't him. Apparently, it was organised by one of your election rivals. They don't like the way Dulane turns their attempts to discredit you back on themselves – those heartwarming press releases about a life turned round and making good despite their dirty tricks.'

'Mr Singh told you all this?'

'No. Two chaps from Homeland Security broke the news to me late last night. Somehow, they had got wind of the plot and suspected your rivals of using you to gain undue influence over my work. They hijacked the kidnap by taking over the old flour mill and ambushing the car. There was evidence your kidnappers intended keeping you a prisoner there for some time.'

'Does Dulane know about all this?'

'He does now. But he didn't when he reported your abduction to the local police this morning. A volunteer from The Drop In saw those thugs grabbing you in the street and making off with you. Dulane has also agreed to letting you have a few days off to get over the attack. It'll give the police a chance to find some evidence against the plotter while you're not around.'

'So that's why we're not heading back to Paddingham. Where are you taking me?'

'Up to your grandma's for a few days. I can only stay overnight, as I have to get back to the office. But we want you to stay at least a week. And don't contact anyone. I will come for you when the time is right. Perhaps after that, Dulane will appreciate you a bit more.'

I defended Dulane and pleaded to be allowed to call him, but Father was adamant. He even blocked Dulane's phone numbers on Grandma's phone.

And so, I spent the next week in Aldham, hiding in plain sight as Grandma's live-in carer while her usual carer had a holiday. When I took Grandma out and about in her wheelchair, no one saw me. They only saw my carer's uniform: the bright red tunic over my jeans and the matching peaked cap hiding my hair.

It became a special time for us both. The weather was good enough to get out most days, around the shops, in the park, and even to the local theatre for a show. In the evenings, we would turn off the television after the news and talk.

Grandma told me about the old days: what life had been like before the Five-Day War destroyed so much of the world. She had been a young woman then, living in a world of technological advances we can only dream of now. After the devastation, she had travelled with the refugees to the only habitable continent left. So many people came, they caused chaos. Different customs, different beliefs, different ways of living. To end the chaos, the politicians signed the Treaty of the Alliance dividing the continent into three countries, nearly sixty years ago. Grandma chose to settle in capitalist Sidion and worked with the other refugees to recreate here the lands they had left behind.

Grandma's lived experiences of what I had classed as history helped me realise how lucky I was to be living in an age of peace, where politics and diplomacy removed the need for warfare and aggression. How lucky I was too, to be able to take part in the democratic processes which helped run Sidion, however flawed they seemed in practice.

The media reported my abduction the second night of my stay. It was well down the running order: just a brief interview with Dulane at The Drop In. He blamed my election rivals and thanked the people who had rescued me.

'Doesn't that kidnapped politician look a lot like you, Virginia?' Grandma said as I turned off the television.

'Yes. What a coincidence,' I replied. 'Remember you told me last night about meeting Grandad? Shall I fetch down those old photo albums of you both from upstairs?'

She gave me a sideways glance to warn me she knew I was changing the subject but let me fetch the albums, anyway.

Five days later, my father came to collect me.

'You look so much better now, Ginny! You've lost that greyness,' he said as we travelled back to the capital.

 He gave me strict instructions about what to do when I got home – to let his lawyer take me to report to the Paddingham police station first thing in the morning and to tell them the truth, everything exactly as it had happened.

We arrived at Paddingham mid-afternoon. Father let me off near The Drop In, and sped away again before anyone saw him. I looked through the window of my constituency office and noticed how down everyone seemed inside. Little work was getting done. Piles of papers and dirty mugs had multiplied on the desktops.

Then I walked in. The team looked up; their faces lit up at once. They crowded round to hug me, firing questions about what had happened to me. The noise brought Dulane out of the back office. He grabbed my hands, spun me round and gave me a huge kiss. Everyone cheered.

'What can we get you?' he asked.

'I'd love Benson to make me a mug of tea, the way only he knows how.'

The faces around me fell again.

'Benson's been arrested,' Dulane said. 'The local police have charged him with attempting to kidnap you. We must get you to the station right away to get him released.'

'I can't. I'm under strict instructions not to see the police without the lawyer I've been appointed. We've arranged to report to the station tomorrow morning.'

'What? Surely you, of all people, would want to save Benson another night in the cells?'

I felt so torn. But loyalty to my fellow worker and friend won out over obedience to my father.

'OK then. Let's go.'

2:8

Dulane and I walked up Paddingham High Street from The Drop In to the police station as the streetlights flickered on. The four-storey utilitarian building was all too familiar to me. I looked up at its grey concrete façade and vaguely recalled less fortunate times I had been there.

We introduced ourselves to the duty officer behind the plexiglass of the front desk.

'Dulane Ellis and Ginny Lee,' Dulane opened. 'We want to speak to someone about a man you're holding, Benson.'

The duty officer spoke to someone on the intercom and then told us to take a seat. A few minutes later, two officers came out from the depths of the building and introduced themselves as Detective Chief Inspector Smith and Detective Inspector Brown. They showed us into a cubicle-sized interview room off the reception area. Their smiles switched off as soon as the door had shut us in.

'So where have you been for the last seven days, Miss Lee?' DI Brown demanded.

'I've been living with my grandmother in Aldham, looking after her while her usual carer was away.'

'We've been searching high and low for you for days! Why didn't you report to the nearest police station as soon as you were freed?'

'My father reported my rescue by a squad from Homeland Security the same day.'

'And who is your father?'

Dulane answered, 'Deputy Head of the National Bureau, James Lee.'

It was the sort of name dropping I hated, and it didn't have the effect Dulane had hoped.

'And I'm the Queen of Sheba!' Brown scoffed in disbelief.

'Ginny Lee is one of the candidates standing for Paddingham in the forthcoming elections,' Dulane continued.

'Oh, yes! We know all about Ginny Lee. She's had a few tastes of our hospitality here! What are you on tonight? Drugs or booze?'

'Don't answer that, Ginny. Officers, we are here to confirm Benson was not among the men who kidnapped Ginny last week.'

'The Homeland Security squad arrested the three men responsible during my rescue,' I added.

'So you're still claiming you were kidnapped by people you did not know? Even though you got in the black car willingly and went for a jolly in Aldham all week?'

'I wasn't going to ignore an order given at the point of a six-inch knife,' I said.

Brown fired questions at me: how many, what were they wearing, the colour of their skin.

'How many were black?' he insisted.

'None.'

'How could you tell? They'd covered their faces.'

'They didn't have dark brown eyes.'

'Why did they let you go?'

'They didn't let me go. Homeland Security rescued me.'

'Why didn't you make a run for it before then?'

'People do throw knives as well as stab with them.'

And so it went on. The forty-minute interview seemed to take hours. The officers clearly wanted to trip me into making a statement which would incriminate either Benson or me but could not go too far with Dulane present.

At the end of the interview, they let us back out into the reception area. Somehow there, they managed to separate us. As Dulane walked through the airlock-style sliding double front door, I found myself bundled into the building and down to the custody suite. They emptied all my pockets and took me to the cells.

In the corridor outside the drunk tank, Benson was sitting on a bench with an officer beside him. His left hand covered the rip in his jeans as he relived the time before when he was beaten up in that same police station and his friend had died. He looked up at me, his dark brown eyes charged with fear. I reached out and shook his right hand, my pale waxy fingers entwined with his long mahogany ones.

'Do you know this man, Miss?' asked DCI Smith.

'Of course I do. Benson lives downstairs from me. He volunteers at The Drop In, making teas and doing the washing up. We've been friends for years. What's he doing here?'

Smith didn't answer. He just threw me in the drunk tank, where I had slept off a hammering a few times before.

Father's lawyer, Mr Green, got me released next day.

As we walked away, he asked me, 'Why didn't you wait until this morning, as we instructed?'

'They're holding my volunteer, Benson, on a trumped-up charge, trying to pin my kidnapping on him. We need to stop them. Can you help?' I pleaded.

'No. You're not the one who is paying my bills.'

Two days later, Benson's body washed up on a mudflat along the River Heane. He had been beaten to death. The police investigation was perfunctory. It concluded he had been set upon by a rival gang when he left the police station. The thugs must have dumped his body in the river. Case closed.

And that is why we started the new campaign, *This One's for Benson*.

Its beginnings were small. I asked our volunteers at The Drop In to find out if any of the capital's lawyers did social need cases. They discovered the union, Lawyers for All, whose legally qualified members accepted cases of social justice where the little people like our constituents did not have the resources to take on the rich and powerful.

I phoned Lawyers for All with my begging cap on, still feeling sick inside that I had not been able to save Benson. Their receptionist put me through to a young female lawyer called Stacey Foster. Her response surprised me.

'You're the Ginny Lee, of the Paddingham Drop In Centre? What a privilege. What can I do for you?'

'I have a favour to ask. Our volunteer Benson died after being held in police custody on a trumped-up charge. I want the people who colluded in his murder brought to justice. Would you be able to help?'

'Is that the young man who washed up on the banks of the Heane earlier this week? Previously seen last at Paddingham Police Station? Of course we can help. We can't guarantee any results, though. And your volunteers will need to do a lot of the legwork. We would charge our usual flat fee for social need cases – a tenner to establish a contract and make you our legal client. That keeps us both safe. Is that all right?'

'All right? That's wonderful. I thought I would have to work hard to persuade you.'

'We owe you a much larger favour than that, Ginny. Since your Drop In Centre started, our caseload has fallen by a third. All the petty administration cases our assistants had to do because they didn't require legal input dropped by 90 per cent. That's left us more time to handle the big cases where our expertise is vital. We even send people to you for help because we know you won't fleece them.'

I went round to visit her with my tenner that afternoon and told her all the sorry tale. She drafted an application to the court and the coroner's office requesting copies of the case files about Benson's arrest and death and sent me away with a list of tasks for the Centre volunteers to do, mainly information gathering.

As I was leaving, she stopped me at the door and said, 'Ginny, if you're doing this to salve your conscience, you will be disappointed.'

'I was at first,' I admitted, 'but not now. This one's for Benson, and for all the others like him, too poor to count.'

And that's how we got the campaign name.

We started off with an article in the local paper, telling Benson's story and the experiences of three others who fell foul of our local police, those fortunately still alive. A local business gave us a hundred badges with a photo of Benson's face on a blue background and the campaign name diagonally across in yellow lettering. People came to the Drop In with their tales of police malpractice and brutality: we recorded the details and gave them a badge. It took less than a month for all the badges to go.

The left-wing radio station EBC took up the story and asked for some cases they could broadcast. We checked with the originators and Lawyers for All, and gave the station the names of those who had given permission, where it would not compromise possible legal proceedings.

A local printer gave us a lot of publicity material and helped us secure billboard space. I will never forget the thrill of seeing Benson's face and the campaign slogan *This One's for Benson* splashed across the billboard under which, only a few months before, I had sat in the pouring rain clutching an unappreciated box of Wiener's chocolates for Mother's Day.

And then the police started raiding The Drop In. Their warrants were spurious. One time, it was for drugs, another time for weapons, another time for an absconding criminal. They would march in, slam the warrant on our reception desk, herd all the people outside – rain or not – and search our premises, leaving a huge mess behind them. Dulane called the raids 'fishing expeditions'. For people with a past like me, they were a nightmare.

The constant state of alert wore me down after the fourth raid. To cope with the stress, I often sat in the backyard and talked to Mr Singh over a mug of spicy chai. But of course, that was the time Kitty Derrer and her husband Sam chose to come round and inspect us.

42

2:9

The Derrers sat with Dulane and me in our back office. Kitty opened a black file labelled 'Paddingham Election'. It listed everything the constituency office and The Drop In Centre had achieved, together with a financial statement of our income and expenditure since the day Mr Singh had handed us the keys to the shop. I looked at Dulane in alarm. He gave me that reassuring smile of his that could banish my every fear.

'Ginny and Dulane, we've kept a close watch on everything you've been doing here,' Kitty said. 'Your donor is pleased with the tight ship you've run financially. You've achieved great results for relatively little cost. Well done.'

'Who is our donor?' I asked. 'You must have their details for our election expenses.'

Kitty looked at Sam. Then she said, 'It's one of the Directors of The Training Bureau.'

'Not Roul Khoury?' Dulane demanded in concern.

'No. Jean Swift. You won't know her.'

Sam changed the subject. 'Dulane's told us about the police harassment you're now experiencing. That's good. That means you're really needling them. Don't let them put you off. We're getting close to the prize.'

Kitty continued, 'Next week is the time to start the election campaign proper. You and the Centre are well enough known now. Let's turn all those people you helped into votes.'

She told us how to conduct our campaign and reminded us to record all our election expenses. The admin work seemed a mountain to me, but Dulane gave me that reassuring smile of his, telling me not to worry. He would look after the detail, I just had to continue being myself.

As the Derrers stood to leave, Kitty gave us a gentle warning.

'A little birdie told me you two are getting close. Be very careful. The campaign officer has to live completely independently of the election candidate – a rule they brought in after some bad actors fleeced the system two years ago. We want you to keep squeaky clean. So check the premises every night, and no hanky-panky. Don't let anything get in the way of our campaign.'

'Don't worry, Kitty. We'll keep at arm's length,' Dulane promised. His winning smile swayed her too.

With two months to the election, my life became a treadmill of media interviews and appearances. The toughest events were sharing a platform with my rivals, Sal Marchon on a Commercialist ticket, and Eri Arayon on a Liberal ticket. After one particularly gruelling television debate, Marchon hinted at my connections with the underground movement, calling me a Brown Cloak. He was referring to a dubious restaurant on the seedier side of town where would-be revolutionaries liked to hang out in spy costumes. I denied it of course.

Marchon's attack had been prompted by an eruption of cheap litho press posters in the style of the Brown Cloak artists, which showed my silhouette in black and red on white with the tag line, *This One's for Benson – be sure to vote on the 25th*. You couldn't go anywhere in Paddingham without seeing at least five. One newspaper printed the underworld claim. Lawyers for All ordered the editor to show his evidence or print a retraction. The retraction appeared the following day.

Then one of The Drop In Centre volunteers wrote a song lionising me as a New World Hero. The embarrassing ditty followed me about wherever I went during the last weeks before election day. I wished I had the singer's confidence in me. So much had happened in such a short time, it all felt too unreal. When I went home each night to my little *pied-à-terre* bedsitter and sat in the worn old armchair, the razzmatazz and the fame seemed like some strange hallucination.

The day before the election, we worked relentlessly in our final push. I gave four different speeches: at a business lunch, a televised rally, a tea club and a formal dinner. Opinion poll results came flooding in from the different wards. At first my chances looked poor but then improved. In the end, it looked as if all would depend on the weather next day. Winter had started early that year: Snow was already snarling up the Eleter traffic systems and might stop the electorate going to vote.

'Lucky our voters don't have cars,' Dulane said as he compared the poll forecasts.

'As long as it's not so snowy they all stay at home,' I said.

'While you're monitoring the polls at the office, all our volunteers will be out persuading every last one of our supporters to go and vote.'

The unreal effect stopped on election day. The Drop In Centre workers put in an exhausting shift drumming up support and ferrying people to the polling stations, while I manned the phones and received the fluctuating results of the exit polls. At 9 pm, I joined the other candidates at the local government offices ready to observe the count.

My rivals, Sal Marchon and Eri Arayon were complacent.

Arayon explained to me, 'You've got to have a ticket. Marchon and I both have tickets. People vote for us because we represent our parties. But you? No party. How can you expect to win?'

'Oh, she's on a ticket all right,' Marchon said. 'Paid your Brown Cloak dues, Miss Lee?'

'Doesn't exist,' I replied with more confidence than I felt.

The doors to the polling stations closed. Half an hour later, the ballot boxes arrived in the counting hall. Our volunteers and party supporters joined us there. We watched from a raised platform as the vote counters fed completed voting slips into scanning hoppers. Each voting slip was scanned into two independent computer systems, each with its own deputy returning officer to adjudicate on indistinct and spoiled forms. The system was efficient but took a couple of hours due to the greater-than-normal number of votes cast.

It was about midnight when the returning officer joined the three of us on the platform and asked our volunteers to return to the counting floor.

We stood to either side of him as he called for quiet and read out the results. Marchon had his acceptance speech ready. I had a few notes on a slip of paper: one side gracious acceptance; the other, gracious loser. My pulse pounded in my ears and I was struggling to breathe.

'A total of 39,249 votes were cast, representing a turnout of 69.8 per cent. The number of votes cast were as follows: Ericsen Arayon, 10,567 votes; Virginia Susan Lee, 14,580 votes; Salomon Marchon, 14,102 votes. So Virginia Susan Lee is duly elected to represent Paddingham for the next term of the People's Democratic Assembly.'

I could hardly believe it. With tears in my eyes, I fumbled for my slip of paper with its inadequate few rough notes.

'Bloody split vote!' Marchon muttered, and called for a recount. The deputy returning officer handed up the results calculated by the reserve computer. While these figures were different, they had no effect on the result. The returning officer guided me to the podium.

The acceptance speech I delivered was a shambles. My handful of notes was exhausted in the first twenty seconds. Then I found myself thanking everyone and their auntie. I brought it to an abrupt finish by punching my right fist in the air and shouting,

'This one's for Benson!'

A huge cheer erupted in the crowd. I stepped down from the platform, feeling I had truly arrived.

2:10

We threw a huge party that night. The Drop In Centre was so full, people spilled out onto the high street. It had been a long time since Paddingham had had anything to celebrate, so we made up for it.

Nahal Singh did the catering unasked, as his way of congratulating us. When I thanked him, his reply stuck in my mind like a thorn you can't get rid of.

'You have done well to win this seat, Miss Ginny. But don't think your battles are over: they have only just begun.'

The following Monday, I joined 136 other representatives at Government House in Eleter to be sworn in to office. The only other item of formal business that day was to elect the President from the body of representatives. With the Commercialist Party winning the majority of seats again for the fourth time, their party leader Simon Falley won the vote by 74 Commercialists for to 63 against, made up of 51 Liberals and 12 independents like me. The Commercialist margin was narrower than it had been, but not enough to worry them.

The first day included an induction tour of the premises and a talk about procedures for people like me who were new to the place. Our positions as elected Representatives included free office space in Government House for those who lived further away. As my constituency office was only four miles from the Chamber, I chose to work from there instead, giving me an additional office subsidy. This easily covered our renegotiated rent and all our service charges. I was also able to claim wages for three workers: an administrator, a researcher and my Election Officer, Dulane. My own salary for the post was so generous, I used half of it to employ a fourth worker to manage The Drop In's caseload and volunteers.

The newly elected Assembly met for business at the start of the following week. It always met in the afternoon and concluded business late evening. We met in the Assembly Chamber, a spectacular amphitheatre with a clear roof, on the top floor of Government House. Simon Falley sat at the central rostrum, with the semicircular tiers of desks behind him reserved for his party. Opposite him sat the Liberals and Independents. My own desk was high up at the back. It had the standard terminal link to the internal computer system for checking in, reading and lodging papers, seeing the day's agenda and close-ups of the people speaking.

My desk had a clear view on my left of the enclosed Observers Gallery and Press Box above the Chamber. A handful of citizens were watching, together with three bored-looking reporters. They looked up with vague interest when their business screen feed reported that I had checked in.

My first action was to lodge five questions for debate by the Assembly, all concerning Paddingham issues about policing, welfare, housing, healthcare, and drug abuse with harm reduction. Kitty Derrer had given me more, but I found I was limited to just five in active process at one time. As I was competing with 74 Commercialists and 62 other Representatives, each entitled to five active questions, mine were lost among the many hundreds.

Each day's business comprised discussing issues tabled for debate. The Representative who had lodged the question spoke in support of it, providing further evidence for the rest of us to look at through our computer screens. A designated Representative from a different party then spoke, usually against the question, after which the matter was opened for debate before a decision was made.

My first question was due to be debated about three weeks after I had tabled it but was put back when the Assembly ran out of time due to filibustering on the previous question which had delayed the vote. When that happened a third time, I understood what Mr Singh had meant. I used a forced debate clause to prevent the question being lost, and finally gave my maiden speech on the last Thursday before the Spring Holiday.

My question raised the issue of police brutality in the capital and the lack of accountability or consequences. By my hand sat a file holding copies of all the reports of police brutality made to Drop In volunteers, in those cases where the victims wanted us to take matters further. I said:

'Honourable Representatives, the question I have lodged for debate concerns a serious issue affecting Paddingham: police brutality. This is not just a headline or an abstract concept but a real experience for many of our constituents, including myself.

'You will already be familiar with our campaign *This One's for Benson.* My friend and volunteer died after being wrongfully arrested for kidnapping me. When I sought to correct that wrong, the police wrongfully locked me in the cells overnight instead. This abuse of power proved fatal to Benson and had a lasting impact on the lives of all who knew and respected him. Unfortunately, such experiences are not unique.

'This file beside me contains more than a hundred statements made by Paddingham constituents about their own harrowing experiences. These are not just stories but documented reports. They speak of beatings, unlawful detentions, and persecution by the local police. They include the use of strip searches for minor offences, including a fifteen-year-old girl who was strip-searched for "smelling like weed"; use of excessive force during arrest and while in police custody; inappropriate conduct towards women, including molestation, sexual misconduct and even rape; and the disproportionate number of deaths of people from minority groups or living in poverty while in custody, like Benson. And yet, in those cases where the victims have tried to take matters further, their complaints have been dismissed: there has been a total lack of accountability or consequences. These accounts highlight a systemic problem that needs immediate and comprehensive reform.

'We must restore trust in our law enforcement, ensure accountability, and make sure such injustices no longer harm our community. Let's move forward with determination and empathy to build a system that truly serves and protects all citizens.'

As I spoke, I could feel the shock of those below me at the opposition desks when I gave example after example.

A Commercialist spoke against the question. He ridiculed my constituency, the victims who had spoken to our volunteers, and the work of The Drop In Centre itself. He praised the work of the police in an area of high criminality and said that criminals always accuse others of their own crimes.

The debate was heated. Several Liberals supported my question and dismissed the objections of the Commercialist who had spoken against it. Others spoke urging caution. The debate ended with Liberal Joe Kinder saying even if only one per cent of the reports were true, the claims made in them needed to be investigated. He proposed an independent judicial review of police procedures in Paddingham, with legally binding conclusions. When it went to the vote, his motion carried 58 to 41. Even some of the Commercialists had voted against their own party line.

Afterwards, I went for a break in the private restaurant. As I placed my order, Joe Kinder crossed to my table and sat with me.

'That was quite a stunt you pulled off today, Miss Lee. You're no novice, are you!'

'Thank you for your help. You swayed the vote for me.'

'I couldn't have done that if you hadn't done your homework. You're not the usual independent.'

'You mean, I'm not a closet Commercialist? Live where I live, and you'd know why. I'm just frustrated I can only lodge five questions at a time.'

'Perhaps we can help.'

He offered me an informal arrangement to vote swap, supporting each other's motions. It was pretty unequal: all the Liberals on his side, just me on mine. I suspected a trap, but he said no: I was fighting for things his party believed in. If I had other issues to raise that were blocked because of the system, he could ask his colleagues to take over those they felt they could support and enter them into the system for me.

I told him, 'That is a very generous offer. Thank you so much for making it. Please don't feel offended that I can't say yes right away. I need time to think it over and discuss it with my agent.'

'Take as much time as you like. Only your constituents will miss out while you do.'

I left the Chamber early that evening. As I walked out into the street, a mob of reporters descended on me, waving copies of the first editions of the evening papers. The issue of police brutality had made the front pages. I answered their questions as best I could before leaping on a bus to escape. After that, when I left the Chamber, I always took a taxi home.

2:11

Kitty Derrer was over the moon to hear about the Liberals' offer. She ordered an emergency meeting at Dulane's house that same night. Dulane drove me down in his big estate car – useful for carrying campaign materials and volunteers, he said. It was the first time I had seen his home. It shocked me to see the splendour he lived in while I continued to slum it in my *pied-à-terre* bedsit in Paddingham. The three bedroom detached villa was part of a small new estate on the edge of Epser, not far from my father's house. Dulane's wages as my agent would barely support the upkeep, let alone a mortgage. I wondered how he paid for the rest of his living expenses.

We arrived about midnight to find Kitty and her husband, Sam, already there. They told us they had let themselves in with a spare key. I began to feel like a spare part. The resentment must have shown on my face, because Dulane told me to cool it.

I told them everything Joe Kinder had said to me. Kitty was all in favour of agreeing to the vote swap.

'Accept it at once! We just need to choose the issues to pass over.'

'But we will lose control of the questions,' I said.

'What we lose in control, we will gain in clout! Fifty-one Liberals backing our causes will give us much greater influence, and you will gain their credibility.'

Kitty went through the list of questions I had not been able to lodge and selected twelve she thought would be supported by the Liberals. Dulane was tasked with reframing them in such a way to pass them on to Joe Kinder with confidence.

Dulane's phone rang while we were talking. He answered it and handed the receiver to Kitty with the cryptic comment, 'The Boss, for you.'

Her manner changed at once. She twisted her hair round her fingers as she spoke, like a coy teenager. The change wasn't lost on me or her husband, Sam. I was still trying to join up the dots while the man spoke on the other end of the line. The realisation came all too soon, when Kitty whispered, 'I will, RK,' and returned the receiver to the cradle.

Her manner became businesslike again as she turned to us to report, 'Our backer says you have made a good job of representing your constituency. Not a penny wasted.'

The colour drained from my face. 'You mean Roul Khoury? The Training Bureau backing is just a front for him?'

I grabbed the list of questions Kitty wanted me to pass on to Joe Kinder and read through them again. Hidden among them were requests to legalise category two drugs, to alter gambling laws and to relax the supply of credit; all of which would benefit the interests of the greatest crook in town and increase his profits from servicing addiction.

I felt sick at the thought of being his catspaw, when so many people I had known had died because of drug, alcohol and gambling addictions.

Dulane saw my expression and leered. 'It's too late to be choosy now, Ginny!'

Suave though he sounded, I knew that was a threat.

'So I have been the gullible fool, innocently fronting The Network for you from the start.'

'No, Ginny. You have always been your own woman. Look at all you have managed to achieve, with a little help from the rest of us.'

I looked at the Derrers' faces in turn. They nodded. They were all his people! All helping me be his patsy! My first thought was to storm out and resign. But I had put myself in a dangerous situation: a minnow surrounded by sharks. Instead, I did the thing I deplored the most and began to act.

'OK. I'm going to pretend this conversation never took place. I'll offer the Liberals the questions you suggest, Kitty, and I'll lodge the other questions as and when the system allows. I'll assume our volunteers are all working for us out of the goodness of their hearts. And I'll try to transform

Paddingham, no matter what gets in my way.'

'That's the spirit, girl,' Dulane said, patting my shoulder like a dog.

The gathering broke up soon after. The Derrers left and drove off into the night. I tried to leave too, but Dulane insisted I stay the night.

It was what I had dreamed of before they had shown me the truth. The dream turned into a nightmare when Dulane forced himself on me. He said the usual things like, 'You want it really,' as if we were in a porno film and, 'You've been gagging for me to fuck you, ever since we met.' And that had been true but not like this.

He proved a greedy, selfish and aggressive lover, assuming that what pleased him would suit me too. I lay back and took it, dreading that I would have to work with this man again tomorrow. When he finished abusing my body, he rolled over and fell asleep.

I went down to the kitchen and drank a mug of tea while deciding what to do next. Understand, I was no dewy-eyed virgin – I had sold my body for drugs many times in my wasted youth and endured worse. But I had created a romantic confection of growing old with Dulane in a cottage with roses round the door and grandchildren playing at my feet. His one act had smashed that brittle fantasy.

I poured the dregs of my tea over his expensive cream sofa, called a cab and went to find refuge with my father.

Dulane did not turn up at The Drop In next day or the day after. The rest of us got on just fine without him. When he did finally arrive, he winced whenever he moved. Father had clearly got someone to sort him out. I hoped it would be enough for him not to trouble me personally again.

2:12

Everything was going wonderfully well by the end of my first year representing the constituency of Paddingham.

My negotiations with Joe Kinder were successful. He took over five of the issues I offered: four from Kitty's list of twelve, and one I slipped in myself about the unequal treatment of the sexes in health, justice and employment. One of his fellow Liberal Representatives was already working on this issue, and we agreed to collaborate in the research as both of us were at an early stage in preparing the issue to present as a formal question. The support of the Liberal Representatives helped my credibility in the Chamber. With ten questions being progressed through the system, I felt I was starting to make my mark in both politics and society.

So that, of course, is when I threw another spanner in the works.

Lots of people had invited me to their New Year's Eve parties, but I chose to go to Mother's, thinking she would ensure nothing untoward happened to me. As usual, only female guests had joined her. They flocked around us to hear Mother's proud praises for all the work I had done in the past year. It was a relief to see that although all the guests around me were dressed in similar fashion, they no longer wore the exact same costume as each other. Mother's outfit was again white overloaded with diamante, and once again she had pinned a delicate orchid on her bust.

Someone handed me a glass of my favourite tipple as we talked. Without thinking, I drained it. As usual, Mother's whiskey had no taste. I downed another. It still had no taste. I tried some food from the buffet table. That was tasteless too. In growing panic, I downed another drink. Then I accidentally looked aside into a mirror over the mantlepiece.

The mirror's reflection showed all the party guests wearing waxen masks, though in the flesh they were not. To my horror, this time, I saw I was wearing a waxen mask too.

I slammed down my empty glass and tried to pull the mask off my face. My fingers could not prise under the edges. I clawed at the grotesque thing, trying to tear it from my face. Seeing my panic, Mother propelled me out of the dining room into her study. She had seen me like that many times and did not want my latest meltdown spoiling her party.

I wept on her shoulder, the diamante biting into my cheek, and sobbed an incoherent torrent of words. As the spate eased, I sobbed, 'I'm just like all the rest now – I wear a mask too!'

'Honey, we all wear masks,' she said. 'That's the way the world works. You're a politician now. You will always have to wear a mask in your professional life. Just remember to take it off again behind your own front door.'

Frustrated that her words gave me little consolation, she called a cab to take me home. I distinctly remember her taking me down to the street and making sure I got in the back of the cab.

'Now, you go straight home and go to bed, and we'll speak on the phone tomorrow. And I'll make sure Mr Sinclair calls you this week.'

She gave the cabbie my address and paid him a note to cover the fare. Before the cab had driven off, she had gone back inside to her guests.

As we entered Paddingham High Street, I said to the cabbie, 'Just drop me off outside Smoky Jim's Bar. I can walk from there.'

But of course, I didn't. I went straight into Smoky Jim's for more whiskey. When the alcohol failed to take away the cold hand round my emotions, I vaguely remember scoring some MDMA. Nothing after that.

About three weeks later, I came out of blackout at Grandma's house. Father had tracked me down and spirited me off there once again, to hide me after another potential career-wrecking spree in some of the seediest places in the capital. The truth came out in our family council of war the day after my self-awareness returned.

It was there that I found out some of the sordid details. Mother and Grandma listened gravely as Father described my bizarre exploits: soliciting to buy drugs, shoplifting, and even ending up on the roof of a department store long after it had closed. I could remember none of it. He could have told me I had robbed a bank and shot someone, and I could not have denied it.

They wanted me to feel remorse. I had a hangover the size of an office block and I was shaking like a shitting dog with the withdrawals. It was all I could do to be conscious. Remorse would come later.

'At least none of your spree has made it into the papers this time,' Mother said.

'That's because Kitty Derrer's husband, Sam, got his "contacts" to limit the damage where possible,' Father said. 'He said he had to pay a woman who looks like Ginny to say she did the rest.'

And all I thought was, 'Great! Now I've got another mask to wear.'

Mother said, 'I spoke to Mr Sinclair about you, Ginny. I was worried when you tried to tear off your face at my party. He asked me if you had been through any recent trauma.'

Father looked at me for permission. I nodded, and wished I hadn't when my brain bounced inside my skull like a squash ball. With everything he had already told them, a sexual assault would add little extra to my guilt and shame.

'A few months ago, Ginny's aide, Dulane, raped her. Ginny came to my house in the middle of the night, injured and traumatised. I gave her what help I could.'

I couldn't help it: I started crying. Big tears rolled down my cheeks for all the disappointment I'd been holding back for weeks. He squeezed my hand to reassure me. Mother and Grandma were appalled. Grandma put her arm round my shoulders.

Mother asked, 'And you continue to work with the man after that?'

'Without him, the entire house of cards would come tumbling down,' I sobbed.

Mother glared at Father. 'James! Do something!'

He did. When I returned to The Drop In, five days later, Dulane had gone, and his place was taken by Jazz, a fiercely dedicated and efficient young woman. Then the stories started coming out about how Dulane had often hit upon the female volunteers. We did not hear what had made him leave so suddenly. There were new people in his house when I was finally brave enough to drive past and take a look.

My family and contacts took other steps to support me, too. While I stayed on at Grandma's, Father arranged for me to move out of my *pied-*

à-terre bedsit into a comfortable house in a better part of my constituency. Kitty Derrer found me a housekeeper to chaperone me whenever the formidable Jazz was not around. Mother organised regular sessions for me with Mr Sinclair, who prescribed some sort of chemical aversion therapy to help prevent further sprees. After the wreckage of my last blackout, I couldn't refuse any of their practical solutions.

I did not return to the Chamber for four weeks. Joe Kinder was not impressed. Without my support, a Liberal issue had failed at the vote. I gave a meek apology, saying I had been unwell. Joe gave me a sideways look with raised eyebrows that told me he had a good idea of the cause, but he said nothing.

So I went back into the real world with two masks on my face.

I was very good for the next few months: playing the part, keeping my nose clean and doing everything expected of me. Joe Kinder behaved like he had forgiven me and let me work with him again. We pushed through some great concessions and even a change in legislation, by using the tricks the party in power used: hiding the controversial parts in the small print and getting the debate and vote deferred to a session held when most of the Commercialists were travelling back to their constituencies, towards the end of the working week.

The manipulation and duplicity sickened me when I cared to think about it. I had always prided myself on my honesty and directness. Now I was turning into just another career politician. I looked back on the heady days of *This One's for Benson* and despised myself.

Nor was everything forgiven. Some consequences of my slip were not revealed until late spring. I came back to my comfortable home one night after a heavy political day to find the house in silence. Usually, the housekeeper would have been in the hall to greet me as I opened the front door. Sensing something was wrong, I hung my jacket on the hall stand and opened the lounge door.

There, in my favourite armchair, sat Roul Khoury, elegant in a light-weight mid-blue suit. The rogue had staged his entry with the confidence of someone who always has the upper hand: handsome, debonair and dangerous. To either side of him lounged his heavies, nonchalantly chewing gum or picking teeth with a matchstick. The image is seared in my mind like a tableau from some gangster movie. I think they wanted me to feel scared.

I didn't act on it. Instead, I asked where the housekeeper was and offered them tea. Khoury ordered me to sit down and shut up. I obeyed, of course. So maybe I was scared.

'You have now been in post for a year, Miss Lee. And you have done a very good job. But you could have done a far better job. You have failed to represent my interests in the Assembly Chamber.'

At first, I didn't know what he meant. Then I remembered the questions Kitty and Dulane had given me to work on with Joe Kinder's Liberals, and how I had quietly dropped the ones to legalise category two drugs, to alter gambling laws and to relax the supply of credit.

He saw the light of understanding appear in my eyes, and continued.

'I recently had to bail you out after your third bender. I will not do that again. If you have another, you're on your own. And know this: I got you into office, and I can get you put out again just like that!'

He snapped his fingers. His eyes burned into mine. I wanted to avert my gaze but couldn't. He finished with a threat to show how he would enforce my compliance.

'All the evidence I suppressed from your other benders will suddenly become headline news. And you know what that will mean!'

I nodded. My thoughts protested that he was the drug baron who reaped the profits from illegal narcotics taken by people like me: he could not have it both ways. But I knew not to tell him that.

He rose to go. The rest of us stood up with him. He walked up very close to me: I could smell his pomade and see the flecks of grey salting his beard.

'One more strike, and you're out!'

He saw himself out of the house.

I stood there, thinking I would show him. I would get totally smashed and trash up his offices and grass up his illegal empire. I would punish him by destroying myself. And when I became headline news, I would let the world know just how he had manipulated me to get a foothold in our political system.

Just as I was about to leave the house for Smoky Jim's Bar, the front door opened and in walked the housekeeper.

'So sorry I'm late. Someone blocked my car in at the supermarket. It took me ages to get his car moved.'

'At this time of night?' I asked, seeing plots everywhere.

'We had run out of milk. And I wanted to surprise you with your favourite dish for supper.'

So I didn't go to Smoky Jim's. Instead, we sat down to spicy noodles done just the way I like them, washed down with cinnamon tea.

In the morning, I saw the folly of my previous decision to punish Roul Khoury by destroying myself. I threw myself back into my job and tried to ignore the threat over my head.

2:13

The summer term went well politically. I managed to keep my nose clean all the way through to the summer recess. The holiday break did not reduce my workload: it just changed. I opened public buildings, presented awards, visited health centres and libraries and made TV and radio appearances. In The Drop In Centre, I helped co-ordinate several campaigns, including a controversial questionnaire being championed by our centre manager, Jazz.

The Police Conduct Experience Questionnaire was an ambitious project arising from the policing inquiry work we had done through the *This One's for Benson* movement. It had been designed by sociologists at our local university. The questions were arranged in three tiers: a five-minute tick box sheet, a more detailed four-pager, and an open-ended in-depth interview. Jazz had obtained funding for fifty paid volunteers to take the questionnaires out to Network contacts in every shire of the country. Most of the interviewers were sociology students working as summer interns for work experience.

The project really impressed Joe Kinder, who had taken up my invitation to be shown round the Paddingham constituency the day after Government House closed for the summer recess. He arrived as we were finishing the last training session before the volunteers dispersed across the country. When I introduced him to the team, they gave him a positive welcome, knowing how much his mobilisation of the Liberals had helped us win gains on several of our issues.

Once we had sent the volunteers on their way, I took Joe outside to show him round the Paddingham constituency. We were ambushed by Mr Singh, who joined us from the shop next door barely ten seconds after we had emerged. I had told him earlier Joe would visit but didn't expect him to join our welcoming committee.

'Mr Kinder, thank you so much for all the help and support you have given Miss Ginny in the political arena,' Mr Singh said. He proceeded to heap praise on him until Joe raised a hand to stop him.

'Most of the help has come from my party,' Joe minimised, looking embarrassed. 'They see Ginny as a fellow traveller seeking similar political goals to ours.'

Without being asked, Mr Singh took over the constituency tour, giving a non-stop running commentary. We visited the local park, where I had got funding for new safe play equipment; walked through streets of houses of multiple occupancy, where safety regulations were now enforced; passed the local hospital, which now had a new infant healthcare unit; and schools that had benefited from additional funding, as their catchment area was now classified as an area of high social deprivation; until we came back to Paddingham High Street, where once boarded-up shops were now occupied again and a new employment bureau was helping local people find local jobs. It was my turn to minimise my own part in all the local changes. Mr Singh shook his head to stop me.

'Miss Ginny, the day you asked me if you could rent one of my shops, this High Street was dead: the only shop that was open was mine. I had nothing to lose letting you use it for free. But oh, how much I have gained. The people of Paddingham so needed someone to care for them and our little borough. That's what you did. Yes, your volunteers did much of the work, but there would have been no volunteers if you hadn't made that first move.'

His sincerity deeply impressed Joe, who talked about him as we ate lunch in the local café. At the end of our meal, Joe invited me up to his constituency for a return tour. When I demurred, he pressed the invitation by reminding me I was allowed to have some time off.

'Cierte is a great place for a holiday: country walks, fishing and our annual show. I can get you a special discount for a stay at our top healthtel, The Lakeland Hydro.'

Paranoia swept over me as I heard that feared word 'healthtel', so often suggested to me by Mr Sinclair, the psychiatrist Mother paid to look after my mental welfare. Joe saw my suddenly ashen face and gave a reassuring smile.

'The Hydro is a spa hotel: it caters mainly for holiday guests. There is a separate wing for those who stay for medical treatment: they wouldn't disturb you.'

I made an excuse about checking when my diary was free, to give me time to ask Father and Kitty Derrer whether they thought it would be appropriate for me to go. They were both delighted, as was Mr Singh.

So three weeks later, I drove a hire car to the border mountains for a week-long holiday in one of the best spa hotels in the country. And it was fantastic.

I had never been among mountains: the biggest hills I had seen were the rolling hills near my father's house and the moors above Grandma's. The weather was kind. I went for long walks in the countryside and tried my hand at fishing and climbing. I explored the local town and loved the friendliness of its people.

Cierte looked prosperous, with its range of shops around the central square, the traditional stone houses in its suburbs, the Neo-Palladian style town hall and police station, and the undefaced statue erected as a tribute to the Cierte Mountain Rescue team. The constituency looked like Commercialist territory, so why had it elected a Liberal? I asked Joe after he had opened the Cierte Agricultural Show and was escorting me round the competition winners and the craft stalls.

'It's easiest to show you,' Joe replied.

Later, as the show was coming to its natural end, we left the ground on foot and headed back towards the centre of town. Joe took me away from the main thoroughfare to some back streets I had not noticed before. Here were the seedy hotels and houses of multiple occupancy so familiar in my own constituency, just made of stone instead of brick. Then he took me to his constituency office in a side street off the main square.

'We have rural poverty too, as well as urban,' Joe said. 'There are only two industries in this area – farming and tourism: both seasonal work with depressed wages. The spa hotels have diversified into healthcare, so some do stay open all year round. But our wealth is mainly a façade.'

He told me how the area had originally been Commercialist with an absentee Representative who had padded his expense account. Joe had been the lucky Liberal candidate to stand in the election just two months after the scandal had broken.

'Like you, Ginny, I opened an office, took time to listen to people's problems and helped them solve them where I could. My family had lived here since the Treaty of the Alliance, so people knew they could trust me. And they have continued to elect me ever since.'

'Such political stability is very rare. Your wife must be pleased.'

He dropped his head. 'My wife is no longer with us. She had an accident, tripped and fell into the path of a grain lorry. It wasn't the driver's fault: she was too close for him to stop. She used to drink and use drugs the way you sometimes do. But hers came to be all the time.'

My head dropped too, in shame. He saw my reaction.

'Isn't it time you did something about it, before it's too late? I've heard rumours: your backers will stop supporting you if you go on another bender. Sadly, the Commercialists will have heard those same rumours. When we go back for the autumn session, they'll be trying everything they can to bring you down.'

'I'm doing fine,' I protested. 'I've got Jazz at the office and my housekeeper at home. I don't live in a tenement any more. And I get regular injections that will make me too ill to go on a bender.'

He nodded, as if he accepted my self-justification. 'Just remember the warning.'

He didn't mention it again for the rest of my stay.

2:14

I did take heed of Joe Kinder's warning. It angered me that Roul Khoury was already spreading rumours to undermine my position. I was determined to make sure his allegations did not come true.

My first concern was for the police questionnaire. Towards the end of the summer recess, a steady stream of completed forms was being processed by the university sociology department on its mainframe education computer system. Copies of the forms then came to us at The Drop In Centre, where Jazz collated them herself and drew up graphs from charts compiled by hand. She did not fully trust the university staff because their establishment received government subsidies. After she had finished with the questionnaires, I locked them away in a filing cabinet in Mr Singh's shop.

My return to the Assembly Chamber produced a lot of whispered gossip behind concealing hands. It was exhausting to be on guard all the time and to make no mistakes. I took care to eat and drink only food and beverages I knew were safe.

And then the code black message came through.

It was a fine late autumnal morning. I was working with some volunteers in The Drop In before going to the Chamber, when we received the alert. Jazz took the call. Her face blanched.

'The Network has ordered us all to evacuate to the border mountains. The Ouslauv Network says their agents in Anoeth have uncovered a plot to destroy Sidion and Ouslau. Anoether troops have been massing on the borders prior to a missile attack in approximately four days.'

'Are you sure it's genuine?' I asked.

She nodded. 'The code protocol was correct. If we want to save ourselves, we must flee for our lives.'

As we spoke, another volunteer ran into The Drop In: Kaido, our main receptionist.

'Have you heard the news from The Network?' he demanded.

'Yes, Kaido. Help me phone round all the volunteers,' Jazz said.

'Don't leave messages,' I ordered. 'We don't want anyone outside The Network to know in case they attempt to stop us. Once you've tried to contact everyone else, you're free to go. Save yourselves.'

'What about you?'

'I have to stay. I must turn up at Government House as if nothing has happened.'

'Then I will stay with you,' Kaido said. 'Someone has to cover this office while you're there.'

His offer humbled me. I felt so grateful not to have to face the next few days alone.

I went to Government House as normal and listened to the speeches. How pointless debates about things like increases in fuel duties seemed when we could be dead in less than a week. During the meal break, I was sitting playing with my food when Joe Kinder came over.

'Cheer up, Ginny – it might not happen.'

I gasped in brief panic, thinking the secret had got out and he knew. Then reason kicked in as I realised his comment was just an awful coincidence. I gave him some appropriately mundane reply.

It was different two days later, when Joe sat down at my refectory table again. His face was screwed up in concern.

'Why are half your volunteers invading my constituency, Ginny?'

'So that's where they've gone!' I answered, keeping a light tone. 'They probably heard there's a gig on.'

'It's serious. Winter's come early and we don't have accommodation for them all. If they camp out, they'll freeze to death.'

'I'll see what I can do.' This amounted to leaving messages at Roul Khoury's office and the Brown Cloak Restaurant, which never got returned. We had no other ways of contacting the people who had fled as none of them had left a forwarding address.

Then reports of killings hit the news. It wasn't clear who had started it, but the police and citizens turned Cierte into open season for 'vagrants'. Among the dead were several volunteers who had worked on the police questionnaire, including our own precious, dynamic force of nature, Jazz. Kaido and I feared we may have chosen the safest option in staying put.

And then Detonation Day came.

And nothing happened.

It sounds ludicrous now, but at the time I was furious that so many people I had known had died for no reason. I didn't know then about the action taken by the Anoether Network to sabotage the missiles, which had saved a million or more lives, including my own. I thought it had just been a cynical false alarm.

During the winter recess, I returned to Cierte, staying at the Hydro again. It was a trip to mourn my friends and volunteers and to visit the places where they had fallen. I wanted to set up a memorial to them. The local authority refused, fearing that any memorial would become a shrine. The best I could do, with Joe Kinder's help, was get a headstone erected where Jazz was buried. Then I went home, vowing to complete the police research project and publish it in full. The most fitting memorial to that passionate woman whose life had been taken too soon would be to change how society was run.

I enrolled in the university handling the questionnaires to learn how to process the information being sent in by the last researchers still out in the field. The staff reassured me I need not worry about the technicalities of statistical analysis, as the university was using its computer to do that. I persuaded them by saying I would need to understand how the processed results supported the report's conclusions when I presented the findings to the government Chamber and answered questions about it. Copies of everything were still sent to The Drop In Centre, where I continued Jazz's work of collating the interviews by police force, gender and age. The filing cabinet next door ended up with three full drawers of completed questionnaires.

The university published the initial results the following summer. They did not show me their paper beforehand. It was a whitewash. All Jazz's fears had been proved true. How the academics had turned the raw data we had received into the bland report they published was beyond me. Their initial conclusions were that there was no systematic failure by the many police forces, just random actions by some officers who occasionally failed to follow regulations. In response, the university chose not to process the data further and stopped funding the project. The sociology department refused to give me the original copies of the questionnaires or the statistics and administration papers.

I left my last meeting with the project leader, furious. It was clear someone had put pressure on the university to drop the whole thing. They had chosen safety and funding over improving the policing of our country and saving people's lives: people like Jazz and Benson and all those others who had died.

'Kaido, I need to find a computer capable of processing all these questionnaires for ourselves,' I said to him after I got back from the

Chamber the next day. 'The way I see it, there are two possibilities: The Network's and the Government's.'

He smiled broadly. 'I'm ahead of you, Ginny. Let me call my new girlfriend.'

An hour later, a post-grad student called at The Drop In. I had met her previously at the university while I was learning about the principles of investigation – she had been taking the same module.

'Hi, Ginny. I believe you need some help. You can call me Duckie,' she said. Someone less like a duckie I couldn't imagine. With her long mousy hair, ethnic print clothes and worn fur coat, she looked more like an Amber or Jasmine.

I was about to call her by her equally inappropriate real name when she shook her head and put a finger to her lips. She handed me a case containing a memory disk from the university's sociology department.

'You look like you could both do with a break. Why don't we go for a walk?' she suggested.

We headed for the nearby park. Even there, Duckie covered her mouth with her hand or turned to face us close up when she spoke. Kaido continued his boyfriend impression with an arm round Duckie's shoulders and puppy-dog looks.

'The memory disk I gave you contains the raw unprocessed data, the data pool used for the final report, and the final report itself,' Duckie told us. 'Someone massaged the results by removing from the data pool all the reports they considered to be biased – mainly ones where derogatory names for the police were used, and those where the subject was deemed overwrought.'

'They censored them?' I asked.

'There's more than one way to get the results you want in qualitative research.' She spoke as if that sort of thing happened all the time. 'Keep the disk I've given you in a safe place, somewhere other than your office. While you take care of that, I'll run the whole data file through the system and see how different things look. But I'll have to be very careful. I'll be processing it in my access time and I must make sure my own project gets processed too.'

'I'm very grateful to you for offering to do this, Duckie. Why are you risking your degree just to help us?'

'One of those reports is mine, on behalf of a childhood friend. She suffered irreversible brain damage from a baton charge at a peaceful protest march.'

Duckie changed the subject after a brief pause. 'Kaido, are we going to try that new bistro tonight? You still owe me a meal.'

I took the hint and left them to go to Government House. As we parted, Duckie warned, 'Do not lose that data. And do not talk about any of this in your office. Not everyone is on your side and even the walls have ears.'

2:15

We had a break-in a few days later. Kaido arrived to find The Drop In Centre had been ransacked overnight. The contents of all the drawers and cupboards had been emptied over the desks and floor. Far right slogans and fist symbols had been daubed across the walls in scarlet paint.

'Shall I call the police?' he asked me when I walked in.

I looked in all the rooms, discouraged by the mess everywhere. Then I realised there was none of the usual hooligan seal of contempt: no sprays of urine or smeared faeces.

'No, Kaido. They want us to go to the police. Just take photos of each room and then tidy up. See if anything is missing.'

The intruders had got in through a louvred washroom window on the single-storey extension at the back of the shop. I went next door to ask Mr Singh to replace the louvres with a more secure window. When I came back, two of our volunteers, Bob and Janie, were helping Kaido put everything away. A couple of hours later, we all sat at the reception desk, baffled.

'Nothing's gone that I can see, so what did they do it for?' Bob asked.

'Time for a cuppa?' Janie suggested. 'I just need to pop next door for some tea.'

She opened the drawer beside her and took out the petty cash tin. When she lifted the lid, she swore, 'Oh, my gawd!'

In one of the cash compartments lay a syringe part-filled with a colourless liquid. I picked it up to show the others.

'Someone's trying to fit us up!' Bob growled.

An overwhelming compulsion to try the substance washed over me. I felt dizzy and breathless and my body shook.

'Don't even think about it!' Kaido warned me, recognising the look in my eyes.

'I'll get rid of it,' Bob said, snatching the syringe from my hand. He flushed the contents down the toilet and rinsed the syringe several times before crushing it and putting the pieces in a box to dispose of on his way home.

It wasn't enough, though. While I was representing my constituency at Government House that afternoon, the evening papers went to press with a front-page article and a photo of me holding up the syringe. Alerted by a headline on a newspaper stand, I arrived back at The Drop In to find the police searching the premises, legally empowered by a warrant.

Our favourite lawyer from Lawyers for All, Stacey, had got there just before me, called by Kaido to ensure the police did not overstep their remit. As we waited for them to finish, she inspected the newspaper reports with a professional eye.

'This photo has been syndicated, as all the papers have the same one,' Stacey said. 'The cloudy image shows it was taken through your glass window from inside one of the buildings across the road, probably the café. Do you know the people there?'

Kaido nodded. 'They're OK. But they can't afford to vet their customers.'

'The articles are bordering on libellous. I will send a stern warning letter about legal action if they don't print a retraction straight away. We need to reframe the story as an attempt to set you up rather than evidence of your returning to your old ways. What were you doing, holding the syringe like that?'

'I was trying to work out how it had got in our cash box,' I said. 'Then Bob disposed of it. We didn't want to call in the police when we're working on a project that's critical of them.'

The retractions and alternative version of the story appeared in the newspapers next day, but the damage had already been done. What had been whispered as rumours were now discussed openly as facts. The Liberals quietly dropped their support for me and the Commercialists moved to have me removed for being unfit for public service. People pasted adverts over the *This One's for Benson* posters and a parody of the local hero folksong reflected the new 'truth'.

I kept Lawyers for All busy countering every false claim, but it was like playing legal whack-a-mole. It was not clear whether the Commercialist Party or Roul Khoury and The Network were perpetuating the rumour mill. Whoever it was, they undermined my confidence so effectively that I began to doubt myself.

The one thing I still felt proud of was the police questionnaire. Duckie reported to Kaido and me once a week. The data was taking longer for her to process than she had expected because there was so much. She could only run it through the college system at the weekends when no one else was in, which made it harder to disguise what she was doing. When her course leader warned her about her excessive computer time, she had to reduce the processing sessions by dividing the data into smaller data sets, which delayed the results even more.

Then one day, Duckie came into The Drop In with a grave face glistening with tears.

'I've been ordered not to use the college computers any more unless I am supervised,' she said.

We were walking through the local market at the time. The market had just started up that summer and was really popular with the residents. Mr Singh had been none too pleased because it took away some of the custom for his shop.

'What stage are you at?' I asked.

Duckie showed me an ethnic dress on a clothing stall.

'This would look really good on you,' she prompted.

We had done this sort of thing before. I held the dress against my body to check it for size and paid the stall holder. When he offered to wrap it, Duckie pulled a carrier bag out of her student backpack and put the dress inside.

I unpacked the carrier bag in my office later, after she had gone, and found a large folder of printed sheets and another data disk.

The summary of results was chilling: so much police brutality and corruption, so many complaints ignored or worse, followed up with further victimisation. No area of the country was exempt. It was no wonder the authorities did not want this information to come out. Because of their interference, the only person who could write the report was me. But because of computer access, the only place I could put the report together was at Government House.

Duckie had included a useful handwritten plan to help me write up the research. I copied it and burned her original to make sure none of the work could be traced back to her. I also copied summaries of the university computer print-outs and kept the originals in the filing cabinet next door. Armed with only my own work and the notes I had taken when studying the research module at the university, I spent whole days at my workstation in Government House, writing up the research in the mornings and contributing to the debates and votes when the Chamber was in session. I could only engage in constituency business at weekends when the Chamber was shut.

Three weeks later, my own computer use was called into question by the Information Services manager in Government House. He summoned me to his office for a dressing down. As he spoke, I realised he had seen what I had been working on. This was the worst possible news – the only good thing was that I had nearly finished my report. Back at my desk, I printed out a copy for myself and sent another copy to Joe Kinder.

When I went back to The Drop In that same day, Kaido handed me a message from Kitty Derrer: *Doing too much, Ginny: take some time off. Stand-in arriving next week.*

I tried to phone Kitty but got no answer. All sorts of different scenarios raced through my thoughts. I recognised the chaos in my head but had no way to stop it. My only answer was to call on the shop next door, something I had been doing a lot more recently. My pretext was putting the copy of the research report in the filing cabinet with all the completed questionnaires.

Mr Singh looked at me with the compassionate smile of one who knew me better than anyone else I had known.

'Want to talk about it, Miss Ginny?' he asked.

'What is there to say? They are ruining me.'

Tears stung my eyes. All I had achieved in this place of poverty was being destroyed to satisfy the greedy political ambitions of others.

'That is not true. You are doing good here. Your enemies have failed to destroy your political career. So now they try to block your work and use your weaknesses against you instead.'

'They are succeeding.'

'Do not let them, Miss Ginny. Take a step back and ask yourself, who benefits from this?'

I shook my head, too engrossed in self-pity to be able to answer.

Two days later, my adversaries pulled their next stunt. I turned up at The Drop In to find a commotion in the reception area. Kaido was trying to eject a man from the building.

The interloper was Dulane.

2:16

'What are you doing here, Dulane?' I asked. My whole body had gone cold. My mind felt heavy and grey, like lead.

'I'm here to take over, now you've hit self-destruct mode again,' he said. He spoke with the confidence of good backing. His clothes looked too expensive for Paddingham.

'Well, that's news to me!'

I reached for the phone and called Kitty Derrer. To my horror, she confirmed Dulane's arrival was her doing.

'It's just to help you weather the latest storms, Ginny,' she simpered, the lying bastard. I could picture her smirking on the other end of the call.

'You do realise this was the man who sexually assaulted me? He is a predator to any woman who works here.'

'Don't overreact to a little lovers' tiff,' she whined. I bet he hadn't screwed her up the arse.

I hit the Fuck It button.

'Okay. I'm off!' I shouted at her and Dulane, and walked out.

I hired a car and drove up to Grandma's. The weather had changed and it was raining hard. It was a struggle to keep the car on the road and the speedo didn't work properly – it kept telling me I was doing sixty miles an hour when I knew from the way things passed that I could only be doing thirty at the most.

I turned up at Grandma's about tea time. Her usual carer ushered me into her cramped chintzy lounge. Grandma was her usual quietly wily self.

'Have you come to be my carer again?' she asked.

I felt the walls coming in on me and struggled not to run back out of the door.

'Sorry but no: I'm just passing through on my way to Cierte.'

'Then you've come the long way round.'

She said it so simply, as if she were pleased I had thought to do so. But I realised it was really a dig at me for coming up with such a lame excuse.

'Let's phone your father,' she suggested.

My 'No!' was too forceful. She looked me squarely in the eye.

'Your grandfather used to look at me like that, Virginia. It never boded well. Tell me about it, or let it go.'

So much was going through my head, I didn't know where to start. So I said nothing.

I stayed the night but hardly slept and escaped the claustrophobia of her tiny terraced house around dawn.

It was snowing by now, long before my route took me up into the mountains. I stopped at one place to get my hair cut short again. At other stops along the way, I bought a jacket and jeans, a T-shirt and jumper, and a winter coat, all pre-owned. I may have had some uppers and downers too. The many second-hand shops and charity shops in every town saddened me. It showed how our economy only worked well for some.

By the time I reached Cierte three nights later, I had reverted to my old pre-Representative appearance. It felt good to be free of responsibility for a while. I hadn't realised how heavy the weight of everything had been on my shoulders.

The market-square clock rang in the centre of Cierte, calling the townsfolk home at the end of the day. I parked the car on the cobbles and looked up at the lighted clock in the dark. Time had frozen. No one crossed the square. The citizens were all home, watching me through their letter-boxes and their keyholes as they phoned the police.

I drove on before they could pick me up and kept moving until I found Joe Kinder's constituency office in a dingy back street off the square. As the lights were still on, I knocked on the door. A tall horsey woman let me in. Two men stood behind her. I must have knocked too hard.

'Well?' she asked, her arms folded.

'Is Joe Kinder in?' I asked.

'He's not due back for some time.'

'Then can I wait? It's getting very wet and cold out here in the snow.'

'What do you mean, snow? You can't wait here. Mr Kinder is not due back until next week.'

Then I realised they were police stooges. I backed out of the place very slowly, keeping a watch on their every move. They looked at each other and one reached for a phone just before I slammed the door shut between us.

I ran to the car and sped off past the old showground, heading out of town, and didn't look back until I was some distance from Cierte. A police car was on my tail. I slowed down to forty, which seemed like a walking pace, and then found the courage to stop. The police car almost crashed into me. An officer got out and walked to my window. I wound it down.

'Are you aware you've been driving at a hundred miles an hour in a countryside fifty zone?' he asked. Snow was settling on his shoulders and his cap.

'I'm sorry, Officer. I'm from out of town – I didn't realise there was a speed limit here. If this is going to take a while, you're welcome to get in the car out of the snow.' I looked in the driving mirror and saw the mask on my face. It took me all my self-control to stop trying to rip it off.

'Snow? What d'you mean?'

'You – you're in it too, aren't you!'

I put my foot down on the gas pedal and raced off. The police officer leapt back into his car and gave chase. He must have called for reinforcements, though. When I came to a crossroads, the roads ahead and to my left were blocked by police cars. I took the only way free, along a bumpy shingle track lined with snowy pine trees. The track went up into the hills until it circled round a large building, ending at the portico over the massive front doors.

I could not double back because of the police cars behind. Instead, I leapt from my car and ran through the doors into the building.

'Welcome to the Lakeland Hydro Healthtel,' greeted the receptionist.

'Do you have a reservation?'

I froze, realising I had fallen into their trap. But the lobby looked familiar: I had been there before.

'No, I forgot to book this time,' I bluffed.

The doors swung open again to admit three police officers.

'Think she's one of yours, from the Content Wing,' one said.

'I don't think so,' the receptionist replied, checking her occupancy list.

'Well, she reckons it's snowing, and she acts like people are chasing her. She was doing a hundred and ten out of Cierte.'

I stood frozen to the spot, trapped between the strange receptionist in front and the police officer behind. The impasse was broken by the duty manager. He emerged from his office and smiled at me in recognition. My change of gear had not fooled him.

'Miss Lee, we weren't expecting you tonight, but you are very welcome. If you would like to sign the register, I will get someone to take you to your room.'

Responding to his warm welcome, I went to the desk to complete the form. Its request for my credit card details flummoxed me as the numbers kept jumping about on the card. The receptionist checked her system and found the card was already on file.

The manager turned to the police officers with a reassuring smile.

'We will handle things from here,' he promised, and escorted them off the premises.

It felt so normal. I followed a porter into the depths of the healthtel. My room was in a different wing to the one I had stayed in before. It looked just the same as the room in my previous stay, except there was no door handle on the inside.

I discovered this too late, when the door was shut. Trapped in my gilded cage, I checked the window to see if I could leave that way. The descent looked possible, but it was dark and the snow had become a blizzard.

An unexpected tiredness washed over me: I felt as if I could sleep for a thousand years and the bed looked inviting. It was bliss to lie down there and know nothing mattered any more.

The cold winter sun woke me next morning, gleaming through the bedroom windows. I looked out at the view of snow-covered trees and mountains and longed to be on the far side of that view, to find out what came next. It was as if some strange unheard song was luring me there.

The door opened. A young woman entered with a breakfast tray.

'Good morning, Miss Lee. I'm Ashley. I'm your companion this week. Would you like something to eat?'

The food smelled delicious. I turned back from the window to sit at the table she had laid for me.

'I didn't have a companion in my last stay here,' I said.

'Joe Kinder looked after you then. He sends his regards. He told us he received your message, and he'll come and see you when he gets back to his constituency next week.'

'I wasn't planning to stay that long.'

She smiled. 'You're not the only guest to say that. What would you like to do this morning?'

I looked back out of the window.

'Where does that valley go to?'

'Into the heart of the mountains. If you want to go, I'll find us some walking gear.'

Half an hour later, we began our silent walk together along that snowy valley, up through the trees into the mountains. A mist came down. The higher we climbed, the thicker the mist became. The snowflakes were much larger too. And the song was much clearer. I sat down to listen and realised I was alone.

The song was one my heart had heard before: a tune played on a reedy flute against the mournful minor key of some backing horns and strings. When it called me to follow, I struggled to my feet and stumbled on towards its distant piping.

Later on, the mist thinned and the air became warmer. The music led me to a rocky outcrop overlooking a vast desert vale. The brilliant sunshine was so warm, I took off my mountaineering clothes. It felt so good to be free, to have escaped the storms of life.

A distant beam of reflected light showed me where the music was coming from. I climbed down into the vale and set off across it towards this village. When I realised my feet were treading on an army of skeletons, it felt eerie crossing such bone-lands. The skulls made me remember my beloved friends who died at Cierte just one winter ago. I stepped carefully in case it was their graveyard, not wanting to show them any disrespect. Perhaps they have found peace too.

And that is how I came here and met you all. The light has almost gone, the music has ended, and my future is done.

Part 3
Daizin Keberin's Story

3:1

I am not quite sure how I ended up here, but I think it started with the delivery of a parcel.

I had just got home late from work and was preparing a simple supper when my doorbell rang. It was about midnight. As no one was due to call on me, I waited several minutes before answering.

On the mat outside lay a brown paper parcel and an envelope. I reached out a cautious toe to tap the parcel. Its contents felt soft, more like a garment than a bomb. I felt reassured enough to bring it inside.

The parcel sat unopened on my table as I ate, while I wondered what to do about it. I worked as a translator for the Diplomatic Corps, and we were about to go on a sensitive peace mission to Sidion following an incident in Govensh where some temple workers from Ouslau had died. We had been warned to be wary of anything that might have come from a spy.

I picked up the envelope. It bore only my name, written in a hand I did not recognise. The short letter inside was undated and unaddressed. It said:

To my dear child, Daizin;

You have done so well in life that both your father and I are very proud of you. To be travelling with our leader Lebistrom on a peace mission to Eleter! How pleased we are that you will see the city where your father and I were married, just days before we were all uprooted by the Treaty of the Alliance.

Please accept this small gift to bring you luck in your assignment. It is a simple shawl, in the style favoured by our village.

If you have time while you are in Eleter, do visit my dear sister Lois, your aunt. She lives in Hadley Avenue on the east side. Tell her your father and I are fine. Our wonderful Motherland Anoeth cares for us very well, and it would be lovely if she could join us here in Aledion to spend our autumn years together.

From your loving birth mother, Emmy Whitley.

I was astonished. I had never had any contact with my birth mother since I was sent to the Keberin school for the gifted as a toddler, and had no idea what she looked like. As a State official, I could not accept gifts from strangers and was duty-bound to report any such attempt at bribery.

Next morning, I handed the parcel and letter over to my manager. He passed them on to the Special Security Police to investigate.

Two weeks later, I was summoned to appear as a witness at the Special Security Court to testify against Emmy Whitley.

The courtroom was small and bare. The five officials hearing the case, sat at a large table. I stood at a wooden rostrum to give my evidence. Emmy Whitley stood in a larger box, guarded by members of the Security Police. Tears ran down her grazed cheeks. Her gaunt appearance and thin white hair made her look far older than her sixties. She slouched in the box. Her bruised eyes looked vacant. She was no fit comrade to support the Motherland.

My evidence about the arrival of the unexpected parcel was heard last. After I finished, the chief prosecutor turned to address the rebel.

'Emmy Whitley, do you still deny that you made up the parcel and wrote the letter? Handwriting experts have proved the writing to be yours. A forensic scientist has proved that you handled the contents of the parcel. A security officer described finding a surveillance device planted in the shawl. And citizen Daizin Keberin told us how she found your parcel and letter at her door.'

The old woman stared at me with accusing eyes.

'Daughter, how could you do this to me, your mother, the woman who bore you? All I did was send you a good luck gift.'

'Woman, I have never seen you before. My true mother is the Motherland, and my father too. I owe you nothing.'

'But without me, you would not exist! Heartless daughter! Can't you see what the state has done to you? I should have murdered you at birth…'

The Security Police dragged her out of the courtroom. Her curses receded into silence as they returned her to her cell.

The chief prosecutor turned to address me.

'Citizen Daizin Keberin, we commend your loyalty to our Motherland, despite your antecedents. You have helped us foil a rebel plot to sabotage the peace talks. Your actions to protect our Motherland and all who depend on her are an example for all to follow.'

I bowed to hear his praise, proud to have done what I believed was right.

3:2

Our Anoether peace mission left for Eleter in Sidion two days later. I flew with the rest of the diplomatic team in an air force plane. Our premier, Lebistrom, flew out after us in his private jet for the official reception at Eleter airport.

We stayed in one of Eleter's best hotels, right in the centre of the city, but I had little chance to explore at first.

Negotiations were tense, at times frosty. Sidion's premier was trying to broker an accord between Anoeth and Ouslau. The Ouslauv leaders felt aggrieved that our Anoether Youth Police officers had shot and killed four Ouslauv priests during a violent demonstration on the streets of our capital, Govensh. Our Motherland was also accused of contravening Clause Fourteen of the Treaty of the Alliance, which concerned the free movement of people from one country to another. Our diplomats tried to demonstrate that these groundless accusations were just born of economic envy. The other diplomats would not agree with us.

The morning after our delegation had taken over the hotel, we were all surprised by the delivery of armfuls of flowers. The bouquets came as a gift of welcome from Alice, the wife of Sidion's premier Simon Falley. They kept our security team busy for hours. Officer Corrin Alcheth checked the flowers in my suite.

'Bloody awful, isn't it!' she said as she walked in. 'Why can't they just let them grow? Still, it was only to be expected.'

'Why's that?' I asked, and sneezed.

She put her finger to her lips to warn me to be quiet.

'Hay fever?'

I nodded. 'Roses.'

She breezed through each bunch of flowers, removing suspect blooms while I snuffled in the background. After a thorough search, she took all the offending blooms away for disposal, and then came back to check on me.

'Feeling better now?'

'Yes. Why were the flowers to be expected?'

'We found so few eavesdropping devices when we first got here, we knew they would have to appear later. The men received bowls of fruit and nuts instead of flowers. Imagine swallowing an electronic filbert!'

I laughed with her, finding her quite approachable despite her being a security officer. We got to know each other a lot more during the mission.

Negotiations made significant progress over the next two weeks. After the new accord was signed and our leaders had returned home in their private jets, those left of our delegation were granted three hours' leave to see the sights of Eleter. Corrin and I were among the twenty personnel who took the official coach tour of the city centre, and we sat together near the back.

The tour took us past various landmarks, all well-described by our tour guide. They included the temple and palace from the pre-Alliance days, Government House with its Law and Assembly Chambers, the cultural quarter centred around South Kenham, and the zoo with its collection of living creatures saved from extinction in the pre-Alliance war.

As we were turning out of theatreland onto a busy shopping street, the coach gave a loud bang and shuddered to a halt. Our driver got out to investigate and came back after five minutes to order us all off the coach. We saw why once we had all gathered on the pavement. Oil was pouring out of the engine compartment and running down the gutter into a drain. The tour guide instructed us all to wait together in the street until a replacement coach arrived to take us back to the embassy. Corrin and I stood on the edge of the group. I felt very claustrophobic among the noise of the traffic and the rush of the crowds thronging the pavement. Yet Corrin looked more alive. Her eyes shone with the thrill of being amongst it all.

'Isn't it different here! All this life and energy,' she said.

'It's certainly busy,' I replied.

The towering billboards along the streets crowded in on me. I didn't want to smoke that cigarette brand, drink this beer, wear these clothes, or read those magazines. The adverts obscured the beauty of the buildings behind them and the elegance of the architect's original plan for the street.

I looked for a refuge and saw a nearby bookshop. Corrin followed me inside, telling me we should stay with the group. Now it was her turn to feel uncomfortable as she looked blankly at the shelves of Sidionite fiction.

'What are we doing here, Daizin? We must go back to the others.'

'Not just yet. There is something I am looking for.'

I led her through the displays to the section for religion. After a short search, I found a copy of an Ouslauv holy book in a contemporary tongue.

'The Ouslauv delegation keeps quoting from this book. Some of their comments warned me there were nuances I had not picked up in translation. Reading the book in its original language will help me give better translations in the future.'

She regarded me with thoughtful eyes as I paid for the book and stowed it away in my shoulder bag. We went back outside into the mayhem and looked for our tour group. This had dwindled to about five as others had also taken the opportunity to explore nearby shops.

'See, we're not the only ones,' I said, and walked off further down the street.

I can't have been looking where I was going, because an old woman collided with me and fell to the pavement. Corrin helped her back onto her feet while I apologised for my clumsiness. As the woman still seemed unsteady, we helped her walk to her destination, a basement restaurant in a nearby backstreet. The sign hanging outside depicted a masked man in a brown cloak. It seemed an odd place for an old woman to visit.

As we entered, a waiter offered us each a brown cloak to wear.

'What is this?' I asked.

'It is a sales gimmick,' he replied: 'Our customers like to think they are mixing with spies and gangsters.'

I translated this for Corrin's benefit, while the waiter wrapped a cloak round the woman we had brought. A frown crossed Corrin's face.

'But we are not spies or gangsters,' she said. 'I think we should go back to the coach.'

When I translated her reply, the waiter looked alarmed.

'But you will disappoint the lady you came with. Lois wants to thank you for your help, by buying you both a drink.'

Not wanting to cause a diplomatic incident, we sat at Lois's table and ordered tea. None of us had put on a brown cloak. All the other customers had.

'Have you been in Eleter long?' Lois asked us. Something seemed familiar about her, but I could not place quite what.

'We have been here a fortnight, with the delegation,' I said.

I translated our exchange to Corrin. She frowned and kicked me under the table.

'Ask the lady about herself,' she ordered.

I nodded and asked Lois, 'Are you from Eleter?'

'Yes, I live in the suburbs.'

Before I could ask her more, two young men came to our table. They swept back their hoods, shook our hands and sat on either side of Lois.

'Hello, and welcome to the Brown Cloak Club. I'm Bee, and this is Dee,' said the shorter of the two, in a brave attempt at our mother tongue. 'Haven't we seen you before? On the news?'

'You are very observant. We are always at the back in the photos,' Corrin said.

The waiter served our tea and cakes, enough for five though our order had been for three. The cakes were delicious.

'What do you think of Eleter?' Bee asked us.

'It is very exciting. You must love living here,' Corrin answered.

I kicked her under the table to remind her to keep the tone of her responses to official guidelines, and I gave a more appropriate response.

'It is far too commercial. I would love to see your beautiful buildings as their designers intended, not hidden by gaudy billboards and neon advertising signs. The clamour, the greed – how do you live with it?'

'Don't you have things like billboards in Anoeth?'

'We do, but not as many, and they only advertise cultural events and social messages.'

He asked several questions about our homeland which I answered with great pride. Dee asked more questions in their tongue which I answered in Sidionite, while Bee translated as best he could for Corrin.

When we had finished eating we tried to leave, explaining we needed to go back to the coach. Bee had other ideas.

'Some students we know would love to meet you. You clearly love your homeland. It would be a great opportunity to let us all know how wonderful it is.'

Corrin warned me not to miss the replacement coach taking us back to the embassy, but Bee pressed. I chose to let him persuade me rather than her, seeing an opportunity to promote our dear Motherland to those who wanted to know about it.

The two men took us to a place called The Training Bureau about two blocks away in an area of office skyscrapers which towered above the street-level shopfronts. Dee introduced us to all the staff in the reception area except one, who was standing in the back of the room as if he did not want to be noticed. He watched Corrin and me from the back of the reception area with shrewd eyes, like a hawk about to take its prey. His charcoal grey suit and waistcoat fitted his slim elegance so well, they had to be made to measure. He looked the epitome of all that was untrustworthy in Sidion. I wondered who he was.

'We're so glad you were both able to come here for the students' interview,' said the receptionist. 'They are in the common room. They have lots of questions to ask you both.'

Corrin looked alarmed when I turned to translate this to her.

'I think we need to go. Now. Right away!'

I told her not to worry and followed Bee and Dee upstairs to the large lounge known as the common room. Some twenty young students had gathered there. The smell of smoke was on their clothes. They looked like lazy, law-flouting drop-outs with their long hair and their worn ill-fitting clothes. But their minds were keen. The questions they asked about Anoeth had insight. They gave me the impression they wanted to join our Motherland.

Fortunately, I had helped my line manager prepare an information leaflet about life in Anoeth which had been given to embassies to hand out to people interested in migrating to us. I used the same rigid rules as I had used then. Behind me, Bee was muttering to Corrin, translating my exchanges with the students. She frowned more and more, the more questions I answered.

'So your police force is only made up of people our age?' one student said.

'The force that deals with everyday offences like parking misdemeanours, keeping the peace, and other small crimes, yes,' I replied. 'People volunteer to join, and almost everyone does for love of our Motherland. They get paid for their service and are helped in their later careers.'

'What about marriage, living together, things like that? Is it true your society believes in love with no strings?' another asked. His fellow students sniggered, as if they had put him up to asking the question.

'The state approves of people and couples sharing accommodation, as it is cheaper for the state in provision of services. We have no form of marriage ceremony, as it's been proved most people don't want a life-long relationship. Our first love, you see, is Anoeth.'

'They say there's no bars in Anoeth. Is that true?'

'No. Our bars are social hubs where people in the local community can meet and chat and have a meal after work. Since the Treaty of the Alliance, the Motherland has managed to eradicate smoking and drug-taking. It is still working to eradicate wine-bibbing and beer-swilling as these were far more of a social habit. However, statistics show the purchase of alcoholic beverages has fallen sharply over the past few years. If that trend continues, that too will be a thing of the past before the century is out.'

Corrin leapt to her feet and slapped me across the cheek.

'You traitor! You thought I couldn't understand. Bee has told me everything.'

I was shocked. 'What do you mean? I haven't contravened any of the guidance by AR74.'

'What? When you talked about armed strength, airfield positions and migration vetting?'

'But I didn't. Bee must have been translating wrongly.'

'No, he wasn't. Every fact he told me was true. Where else could he get that information but from you? I am placing you under arrest. You're going straight back to the embassy with me. Now!'

She grabbed hold of my arm to drag me away and pulled me to the floor. A scuffle broke out as the students intervened and separated us. Bee hustled Corrin out of the room, saying he would find a taxi for us both.

Dee brought the meeting to a hasty end and asked the students to thank me for coming there. They replied with a muted mutter of a response. He escorted me out of the lounge to a nearby office, where we sat on opposite sides of a desk. I looked back at the door and wondered how to get away.

'Will Corrin know to come and collect me from here, Dee?'

'She's already left to return to the embassy.'

'But you've got to stop her! She's going to report me for giving classified information.'

'Don't worry. She'll think twice about reporting you when she realises how much she will damage her own career.'

I felt too flustered to believe him.

'But all I've done is chat about household matters and everyday living.'

'Have you?' He leered. 'You've done a great job for us. Those students you met had dreams of turning Sidion into another Anoeth. But the picture you painted of your Motherland was far different to what they had imagined. You described a life with no morals other than patriotism. Your lifestyle is completely straightjacketed by regulations: no smoking, no family, no joblessness, no freedom of choice because the state has already made your choices for you – you can only choose to do more, not less. No possibility of becoming rich and living the easy life long before retirement. And to cap it all, whatever is unregulated at the moment, you proudly assured us will be before the first century of the Alliance is out. Do they want to make Sidion a second Anoeth now? No they don't!'

He leered again and added, 'We'll be doing it all again tomorrow, with someone from Ouslau. By the time we've finished, they won't want to go there either.'

'But why? Why do you want to destroy their hopes?'

'That's business. We're protecting our income.'

A student came in with a tea tray. He poured two cups, handed me one, and left again. I drained my cup, thirsty after talking to the students for so long. Dee refilled it.

'What income? I don't understand,' I said.

'People are happiest when free trade brings prosperity to all. So we make sure our young idealists never achieve the uprising they long for. The skill, of course, is making them believe we are on their side.'

I recalled the businessman in the reception area and felt like a fly caught in a web of his creation. As I stared at Dee, my perception began to alter. The painted flowers in the picture behind him seemed to grow through the glass into the room.

'What's happening?' I asked, standing up to touch the flowers with my extremely long arms. 'I feel so wonderfully tall: I can see the balding patch on the top of your head, I can count the dead flies in your lampshades – poor, dead flies! I can read the dusty documents lying hidden on the top of the big cabinet.'

'We're done here. Let's get you back to the embassy.'

He put his arm round my shoulders and took me through reception, past the happy waving staff, out onto the street.

How can I describe that street that evening? The lights were like jewels sparkling on the black velvet brows of the buildings behind. The music of the traffic and the footfall beat of the passersby blended into an exultant song to life, which begged me to join in too. The pavement reached up in love to take my distant feet, while all around, the streetlights glittered and darted like fireflies.

Dee summoned a taxi for me and helped me climb in the back. He paid the driver and instructed her to take me to the embassy.

'This one's for Emmy Whitley,' he said as he closed the door.

And all the dancing fireflies fell to the ground dead as I remembered where I had heard the name Lois before.

3:3

Eight days later, I was back in the courtroom where Emmy Whitley had been tried. The time between had dragged slowly, as I was not allowed to return to work. Instead, I spent hours reading and translating the holy book I had bought the day of my fall from grace.

At first, I just dipped in here and there, to get a flavour of the book. Its archaic language took some time to adapt to reading, time I had aplenty.

The book had many sections, all written by different people. All the writers agreed that there was a deity, though the deity's name was not always the same. I used the word God to translate these different names. The book promised a golden age where poverty was no more, peace reigned and people would no longer cry. But that we already had, I thought, through the Treaty of the Alliance. Then I remembered the students I had met in Eleter: poverty had not yet been eradicated there, so perhaps the other two were not yet true either.

Several of the writers had written about setting prisoners free. That meant little to me, confident that our legal system would find me not guilty through my lack of intent and my mitigating circumstances. Because I had been charged while working for the Diplomatic Service, the court had allocated me a lawyer. He instructed me to plead guilty because I had tested positive for illegal drugs and had been witnessed giving away state secrets. When I insisted I was going to plead not guilty, he told me I would have to represent myself.

The only good bit of advice the lawyer gave me was to pack all my personal belongings in a box and send them to storage the day before my trial. He explained that I would no longer be living in my flat after the verdict, whatever that turned out to be.

The day of the trial came. This time I stood in the wooden dock where my mother had stood, with security guards on either side. Corrin Alcheth stood where I had previously stood. Her cold words as I had come down from the drug-induced high in my Eleter hotel room still chilled me:

'Of course, your career as a translator is history now.'

The head of the five officials at the table was the same man who had praised me for bringing Emmy Whitley to justice. On his left sat my line manager. The other two officials – one man and two women – were unknown to me.

'Daizin Keberin, you are charged on two counts: being under the influence of the hallucinogenic drug sedetal, and betraying the Motherland and the diplomatic mission you were a part of by giving classified information to Sidionite spies. How do you plead?'

'I plead not guilty,' I answered, confident that the judges would exonerate me when they had heard what had happened to me.

The prosecutor listed the crimes I had to answer to: testing positive for an illegal substance, betraying state secrets, disobeying the orders of the Security Police during a diplomatic mission and bringing the name of our Motherland into disrepute. The lawyer for the prosecution provided evidence to support each charge. I was then given the chance to answer them all.

I explained how Emmy Whitley's sister Lois had set me up to be betrayed by some young men, after Corrin and I had gone to her assistance, by getting us to take her to the Brown Cloak Restaurant at her request. The men persuaded us to talk to some students in a nearby college about life in Anoeth. I had been happy to do this, as I wanted these people to know what a wonderful place the Motherland is to live in. As I answered the students' questions, one of the men pretended to translate my answers to Officer Alcheth but gave her classified information instead. A scuffle broke out, separating me from Corrin. Then the other man gave me tea which must have contained the sedetal. It was only a few moments after drinking it that things became very strange.

'The last thing Dee said to me was, "This one's for Emmy Whitley," as he put me in the back seat of a taxi. I came round later, back at the embassy.'

The prosecutor noted my defence and asked Corrin whether she could corroborate my testimony. Corrin's expressionless face as she answered the lawyers' questions warned me to expect little sympathy from her.

'It is true that we went to the aid of a woman called Lois. She fell in front of us in the street and asked us to take her to a restaurant, where most of the customers wore brown cloaks. When the two men Bee and Dee joined us, I urged Keberin to leave with me, but she refused to go. As I had been detailed to watch all who contacted her in Eleter, I stayed with her.'

'Who had asked you to monitor Keberin, and for what purpose?'

'The Special Security Department, following the Emmy Whitley incident. My superiors expected more espionage agents to contact Keberin during the delegation to Eleter, which they did through the men Bee and Dee.'

The blood drained from my face to learn how false a friend Corrin had been.

'The two men took us to a training bureau nearby, and introduced us to the reception staff. I saw the spy master Roul Khoury watching us in the background. They did not introduce him. I recognised Khoury from pre-visit security training about The Network, but did not let on. His presence warned me to be on guard.'

'Why did you not leave there and then, taking Keberin with you? That would have been your first duty,' said the prosecutor.

It was Corrin's turn to go pale as she realised the stance the court was taking.

'I tried, but Bee and Dee persuaded Keberin to stay.' She retold her story, trying to play on the cultural fears of those in judgement over us. No matter how black she portrayed the people into whose clutches we had fallen, nothing sounded a satisfactory response to the judge's questions.

As the prosecution summarised the evidence, it was clear they would have to convict me and Corrin too. It was only a matter of how harsh our sentences would be.

When the chief judge asked me if I had anything more to say after hearing the evidence, I restated my defence.

'I still claim I was set up by Lois in revenge for betraying her sister Emmy Whitley, and Officer Alcheth was an innocent victim of the plot too. Lois used Bee and Dee to destroy my career and my good name, when Bee mistranslated what I said to make it sound as if I was betraying our beloved Motherland, and Dee spiked my drink with sedetal.'

The prosecutor conferred briefly with the judges and came to a decision without leaving the room.

We were both found guilty of crimes against the state. Both of us were stripped of our privileges and positions: we only avoided deportation to the hard labour camp in Pentern because of our previous good character. The court sentenced each of us to one year's solitary confinement in Govensh prison, after which we would re-enter society as labourers.

The judges stood down. Corrin and I were escorted out of the courtroom to separate cells. I never saw her again.

3:4

I served my year-long sentence in complete disbelief at how I had got there, shocked that the system I had served and respected all my life had treated me so harshly. Every day of mind-numbing repetitive toy assembly in a segregated workroom, I wondered whether I could have saved myself by presenting my case in a different way. I still could not believe that the Motherland was at fault: it had to be through my own mistakes that the court had not recognised my innocence of intent. And I was horrified that my innocent actions had resulted in Corrin receiving similarly harsh punishment, when she had only been carrying out orders to stay with me and identify all who had contacted me in Eleter.

Each evening, before sleep, I had an hour's free time to read, write letters and reflect. I had no one to write to, and all the permitted reading matter was re-education material about the sort of lifestyle the Motherland expected of me once I was released.

Instead, I spent hours reflecting. Often, those reflections revisited the passages I had translated in the holy book. In my changed circumstances, I recalled several of them vividly, even though I no longer had the book they came from or my translations.

At the centre of the book was a collection of poems and songs written by a soldier. He told of his intense loneliness and the many hardships and setbacks he had endured, but he claimed always to feel better when he had talked to his god about his situation and praised the deity for being in his life. His poetry helped me identify a deep loneliness in my heart. But I had no god to help me carry my burdens of isolation and self-doubt.

Another story I recalled from the book told of three men sentenced to burn in a furnace because they would not renounce God, yet they did not die in the flames. I had found that far-fetched when I had first read it. Now, I reinterpreted the story as a metaphor for living through an ordeal.

The passages in which writers spoke of setting prisoners free now spoke to me as I sat on my board bed in a cubicle of a room with a small barred window placed so high in the wall, I could only see the sky. I felt broken. To trust that a deity knew my predicament and wanted me to be free offered me a hope that was too far from my experience for me to grasp.

Eventually, the day of release came. The woman who had escorted me to my cell a year before led me away to a small office to process my release papers. She offered me a room in a hostel and a job on an electronics assembly line, which I accepted. After a year of having all my decisions made for me, it felt right to have those two decisions made for me too. It had been my poor decision-making which had got me there.

I remember sitting in the hostel's café that first evening, totally lost. Other people came and went around me, laughing and joking with each other, choosing meals from the counter and sharing tables. I felt as if I had forgotten how to speak. I would have gone back to the safety of my room without eating that night had someone not taken pity on me.

An old man sat down at my table. He had a lined and weathered face, bleached blue eyes, and an unruly halo of thin white hair.

'I'm Segan the Carpenter,' he said, offering his hand.

'I'm Daizin, the … labourer.'

'What are you going to have to eat? The vegetable and dumpling stew is always a safe bet – there's very little meat in the chicken and leek pie.'

'I'll have the stew, then.'

He persuaded me to go to the counter with him and ordered his meal first to show me how. As the food was charged to our rooms, we did not need any money.

Segan took me under his fatherly wing, helping me find my feet in those first few months as I ventured back out into the real world. Segan helped me retrieve the box of possessions I had packed the day before my trial. How small and insignificant they looked: a few clothes, a favourite mug, some books and papers and, of course, the holy book. He raised his eyebrows when he saw that among my possessions. It was after then that he opened up about himself.

Segan had originally come from a small town in the hills, Entelliard, at the base of the Liarden pass, about seventeen miles from the border. His father and grandfather had both been carpenters, and he was very proud of the skills passed down to him through his family.

'Alas, the love of craftsman's work has all but disappeared with these newfangled modern methods,' he told me once. 'It's just love for the Motherland now, for its goodness caring for all the children. What the children don't realise is that without the state, their mums and dads would have cared for them. They would have taught them a lot more about love and friendship, too. Tell me, have you ever loved someone?'

'No. I love the Motherland. Or I did. Or...'

We were strolling in the nearby park at the time, enjoying the sunshine on our rest day.

'I know, you loved the Motherland until it showed you its fangs. Have you noticed how our country is run by the young, with just a handful of elders in control at the top?'

I had not noticed until his remark drew my attention to it. When I looked back, it shamed me to see how blind I had been.

'Yes,' he said. 'Only a few make it through the treacherous path of life to success. We're just two of the many who fall by the wayside: just collateral damage as our perfect state pursues its ambition to take over the whole world – what's left of it!'

I stumbled in dismay to realise all I had misunderstood before. Our wonderful Motherland, created by the people for the people, did not serve those people at all. In just one generation, the ideals which had founded the Motherland had degenerated into a tyranny of the worst kind. My fall from grace was just collateral damage in a quest for world domination. Brash materialistic Sidion had been hell, but this was far worse. Oh, how I now regretted bringing Emmy Whitley to justice. Even worse, the judgement I had meted on her, Corin had meted on me, and had I been in her shoes, I would have done the same.

Segan guided me to a nearby bench to sit and regain my composure. In response to his sympathy, I told him my own sorry tale, despite fearing he might never speak to me again. But he just patted my hand in a reassuring way. Then he told me about his own crimes, taking messages over the border near Entelliard.

'They found me guilty of espionage and drug running. I was just a courier, carrying letters and small packages – birthday cards and little presents. It wasn't my fault the new national borders in the Alliance sliced communities in half: families and farms riven apart. I just helped people keep in touch.'

We walked back to the hostel. When we said good night after supper that evening in the café, it was the last time I saw him. I asked about him the next day, but no one knew anything. The carpenter had joined the ranks of the Disappeared, probably because of his contact with me.

When I knocked on Segan's door later that week, a new tenant called Esterin opened it and walked into my life.

3:5

Esterin had the reputation of being a firebrand and rebel in the hostel. I found him exciting and challenging. I listened to him for hours as he discussed all sorts of political and philosophical ideas. He loved my ability to read and understand all the major languages, and got me to translate his favourite works from their original texts.

We used to walk for hours in the city parks, talking, exploring ideas, creating ideal worlds for the future. Funny, though, that we never really talked about our pasts. We hired bicycles on our days off together and cycled in the country from dawn to dusk. Time flew when we were together, and I never wanted it to end. It felt natural to become lovers. One of our dreams was to share a flat together once we were free to leave the hostel. We even talked about applying to have a child. Those were heady days.

I wove him a bangle made of my hair and gave it to him as a keepsake. He gave me a pressed flower in return.

'A daisy for my Daizie,' he said as he gave it to me. The flower sat between the pages of a poetry book entitled *Lost Voices: The Pre-Alliance Poets*. This was an underground publication, proscribed by the Motherland authorities. I asked him where he had got it from, but he just smiled.

'I have my contacts,' he said and would say no more.

So perhaps it was no wonder that he, too, disappeared. I had never felt grief like it, even more than my grief over losing the status of my previous career. I remembered what Segan the Carpenter had said about love and decided that must be the cause of my pain. It was the same hurt I had seen in Emmy Whitley's eyes when my testimony had convicted her in court.

I tried to find out what had happened to Esterin. Just as when Segan disappeared, no one could tell me anything. I feared my friendship, or that hostel room, was jinxed.

The last place Esterin had told me he was going to the day he disappeared was to the library after work. We had been regular visitors there, and the staff knew us both well; but when I asked them if he had been there, they checked their records, shrugged and shook their heads. I searched for him in all our other haunts. Those who knew us had not seen him. The rest of the world did not seem to care.

Two days after he had gone, another new tenant moved into his room. He dumped Esterin's possessions in a skip at the back of the hostel to make room for his own. I managed to rescue Esterin's notebooks just before a tipper took the skip away. That night, the TV news showed the image of a body that had been pulled out of the river. It was Esterin. I hugged his notebooks to my chest and wept as my last hope had gone.

My time off became a morbid round of visiting the places Esterin used to go when our shift patterns stopped us being together: the park, the gym, the museum. His notebooks told me of another place too, the Ouslauv temple. His spidery handwriting had recorded at least a dozen visits there. The first visit had been shortly after the Youth Police had gunned down the Ouslauv priests during their ritual procession, the incident which had caused the sending of the diplomatic delegation to Eleter that I had been a part of. I visited the temple complex on my next free day.

The temple was a remnant from pre-Alliance days when Ouslau still possessed the whole continent. The turreted white temple building stood in an extensive and ornate garden full of trees and flowers and statues. It felt like being in heaven on earth, not the false heaven that I had felt when under the influence of sedetal but a real place made of stone and plants and water and the heady scents of exotic blossom. A legion of volunteers worked among the different bowers to maintain such beauty. They all looked elderly, born in pre-Alliance days.

I sat on a stone bench in a secluded arbour and listened to an unseen fountain playing beyond a screen of sweet-scented mock orange trees. A copy of the holy book rested on the edge of the bench, untouched. I dared not open it in case someone was watching. My eyes closed and a peace I had not known before stole over me.

'May I sit with you?' a woman asked.

I jerked awake and looked up. A temple priest stood before me, wearing the traditional long black day-robe of her order. Her straight black hair was tied back from her tawny, smiling face.

'I'm not in the way, am I?' I asked, flustered.

She shook her head to reassure me and sat down near me on the bench in companionable silence.

After some time, a temple bell tolled, disturbing us.

'Do I have to go now?' I asked.

'No. The bell is just letting us know a service is about to start. You are welcome to join us inside.'

I thanked her but declined. She nodded in farewell and walked away.

That evening in the hostel, I regretted not asking her about Esterin but felt conflicted. Despite her friendliness, I mistrusted her: the last friendly foreigners I had met had destroyed my career.

Yet on my next day off the following week, I returned to the temple gardens and sat in the same place. The arbour felt less peaceful this time because I half-hoped the priest would sit with me again. The holy book was still there. I opened it as I waited and read the story of a queen called Esther, who saved her people from extermination.

'Do you understand what you are reading?' asked that gentle voice I had half-hoped to hear.

'Yes, I used to be a translator, so I understand all the words. Why is this story in your holy book when it doesn't mention God? All the other stories do.'

'Those who heard the story in the past knew the presence of God is implied. God placed Esther in a position where she was able to stop the massacre of God's chosen people while they were in exile in a heathen kingdom. Her faith in God gave her the courage to risk death as she asked to speak with her husband, the king, on behalf of her people.'

'You mean we're all like pawns in God's control?'

'God allows us the freedom to choose. Some of us give our lives back to God in thanks. What are you seeking, that brings you here again today?'

I paused, not sure whether I could trust her. Then I remembered how I had regretted not telling her my purpose on my previous visit.

'I come here to remember Esterin. He died not so long ago. This is where he used to come.'

'Would you like me to ask about Esterin in the temple for you? Then, when we meet here again, I can tell you what I learn. Ah, there is the bell. You would be very welcome to come to the service with me today.'

I shook my head, not wanting to take part in a ritual Esterin used to call little more than an acted-out folk memory.

She nodded in farewell and glided off down the path towards the temple. I asked her God to make her enquiries successful.

Circumstances delayed my return to the temple gardens. I had passed my probation and was allowed to move to a one-room studio flat. Its advantage was that I was no longer monitored day and night. Its disadvantages included having to shop for ingredients and cook all my own meals, and no longer living next door to where I worked. Thus, it was two weeks before I sat on the stone bench again and listened to the water playing in the fountain nearby. The mock orange flowers had died and lay in a browning carpet below the trees.

The priestess joined me an hour later.

'I feared we wouldn't see you again,' she said with a smile.

I explained about moving out of the hostel into my new flat but then wished I had not because it told her I had served time. This did not discourage her, though. She suggested we went to her little office to talk, as the autumnal garden felt cooler. I agreed, relieved that she did not expect me to enter the temple itself – that would have been a very fast route to becoming one of the Disappeared myself.

She took me to a room in the administrative block built at the back of the temple complex. The room was simply furnished, with a small shrine on the east wall, a desk with three office chairs, and two worn armchairs beside the biggest bookcase I had seen outside a library. We sat in the armchairs to talk.

She invited me to call her Sister Sontell and asked me my name. When I replied, 'Daizin Keberin', she nodded, as if she had already known my name but was testing me.

'I shall call you Sister Daizin. Here, we are all equal before God. Some of us just have a little more responsibility. Tell me about Esterin.'

I looked away in resentment, having expected her to tell me about Esterin, not me tell her. My eyes focused on the titles of the books behind her right shoulder. Between works about faith and scripture stood a slim volume with Esterin's name on the spine. Tears sprang to my eyes. I reached across to take the book from the shelf. The priestess smiled, as if I had passed another test.

It baffles me still, what happened next. Somehow, the manner of this gentle woman made it easy for me to trust her. Despite all the damage foreigners had caused me before, I cradled Esterin's book and told the priestess all about my relationship with him: our hopes and plans, our studies and our debates. My eyes stung with uncried tears as I spoke. I ended by asking if I could borrow the book.

'Sadly, no. It would be too dangerous for you. Esterin came here to write this. He knew your hostel rooms were wired, so he took care to keep you safe in case your rooms were searched. He loved you very much.'

'So he really is dead.'

She gave me a sealed envelope. It had been addressed to me by name in Esterin's spidery handwriting. My hands shook as I opened it.

Dear Daizie, if you are reading this, I have become one of the Disappeared and you have looked hard to find me. Thank you.

I had planned to move to the border region to become a courier in Entelliard, like Segan the Carpenter had been. I had hoped to take you with me so that we could live a wonderful new life together, the way couples were always meant to live.

Now that I am no longer here, would you be willing to take my place? To go to Entelliard and become a courier? You are uniquely equipped for the role. It would be dangerous, but how important the work would be! No more assembling toys and living in shoe boxes! Wide open spaces and the fresh country air instead, with work aplenty on the farms. Please say yes.

Your very own Essie.

I sat still for some time, looking at the letter. So many thoughts raced through my mind, it was hard to keep track of all the different strands. Eventually, I put some of them into words.

'I would so love to go, Sister Sontell. But I can't. Emmy Whitley came from Aledion, which isn't far from Entelliard, and I betrayed her.'

'Dear Sister Daizin, you betrayed Emmy Whitley because you didn't know any better. If we can make that right for you, will you go?'

I hesitated. Esterin had asked me. But could I trust this gentle woman enough to take that risk? I gave a tentative yes, not realising what it would mean.

Then the priestess dropped the bombshell. 'Because you have said yes, you must leave tonight, to ensure no inadvertent word or deed betrays you.'

That meant the little studio flat I had spent two weeks getting ready to live in would go. Was I like Queen Esther, uniquely placed to help her people in this way? I had only known city life and living on the right side of the authorities. Now I was being asked to put all that behind me. All I had to trust was the belief in Esterin's letter that I could be like Queen Esther, too.

Sontell allowed me time in the temple gardens to reflect. I still didn't understand why Esterin had spent so much time at the temple, when he had plenty of time for philosophy and politics, but little time for the multi-faith beliefs of Ouslau, which this temple represented. In the end, it was the memory of Segan the Carpenter and his stories of service in the borders that convinced me, the thought of helping communities divided by political boundaries to keep in touch.

So Daizin Keberin became one of the Disappeared, and assistant Nurse Plover joined Sister Ansell's mercy mission to help refugees in a border town near Oucern. The temple sorted out my new identity, my papers, and my disguise. They replaced all my clothes, even my purse and my copy of the holy book. I left Govensh two days later in a minibus with seven Ouslauv priests and support workers.

The news reported Daizin's disappearance as a footnote to a piece about the disappearance of a more famous activist. It was a relief to say goodbye to her and the old way of life she had represented.

3:6

The team of people travelling with me were great fun. I had expected religious people to be solemn and profound all the time. Instead, they laughed and joked, and the journey passed quickly with their banter. They improved my Ouslauv idiom no end. By the evening of the second day, I joined in the repartee, though my attempts at humour usually fell flat.

The road blocks to control the flow of traffic in and out of Govensh and other towns on our route were no problem. Our driver gave the Youth Police our travel permits to check we all looked like our photos. They heard us all speaking Ouslauv, handed our permits back without a second glance, and waved us through, barely giving us time to drive off before they beckoned to the next vehicle in the queue.

Our minibus broke down on the third morning, soon after we set off. We were in hill country by this time, travelling along narrow winding roads between remote fortified towns and villages. I had never seen such beautiful surroundings as those rolling forested hills in all their autumnal glory. While others talked about broken axles and how to get help, I sat on a rounded boulder and immersed myself in the view.

A fresh minibus arrived about lunchtime. By evening, our new driver had brought us to Entelliard, the first driver having stayed with the broken-down bus. We found lodgings for the night at the village inn and sat down for what would be my last meal with the team.

The food was unremarkable – some spicy stew with a lot of vegetables and little meat. As I worked my way through my plateful, a familiar voice made me look up. But when I saw the faces of the land workers standing at the bar, I did not recognise any of them.

'Esterin?' I asked, bewildered.

One of the land workers looked me in the eye and winked. My heart stood still. I hardly knew him, he had changed so much. I stood up to go to him but Sister Ansell pulled me back down.

'Later,' she said in Ouslauv. 'We must do the handover when it is safe.'

She made me wait with her party until late evening. It was midnight when I went to my room for the night. The real Nurse Plover was waiting there for me. We swapped clothes and identities: my nurse's robe for her worn shirt, trousers and coat. I emerged looking like a local farmer, carrying the papers for Yenner Devlin and a much plainer copy of the holy book.

A door opened as I walked down the corridor. Strong arms grabbed me and pulled me inside. Instinct made me resist the restraint until my nose recognised my captor.

'Esterin!' I cried, and wrapped my arms around him.

He silenced me with a forceful kiss and closed the door behind us. When he released me, he put a finger to his lips to warn me to make less noise as it was late. Then he cradled me in his arms. I hugged him so tightly, I did not want to let him go, ever.

'Oh, my dear Daizie, I have missed you so much,' he said.

'I've missed you too, Essie. Why did you leave me so? I thought you'd died.'

He explained how The Network had warned him he was about to be arrested by the Youth Police for publishing his book. Had he not disappeared, they would have arrested me too. My grief at his death was the only way he could convince the authorities he had really died – they would have known had I just been acting. Sister Sontell then helped him prepare a way for me to join him, if my love was greater than my fear.

At first, I felt furious that others had planned all this for me without my knowledge or agreement. But then I recalled Sister Sontell's questions. She had let me choose. I had agreed to go in Esterin's memory, not knowing my 'yes' would take me back into his arms.

We stayed in that room until morning, sharing a bed together for the whole night. Having thought I had lost him forever, it was bliss.

After breakfast the next morning, Esterin and I walked out of the village, taking the road towards the border, through thick pine forest. It was pouring with rain, but I didn't care. I was with the one I loved, and we were walking together towards our wonderful new future.

Two hours after we set off, a cattle truck stopped to offer us a lift. Esterin saw a yellow pennant on its bonnet and opened the door for us to climb in.

The driver was an old farmer: thick-set, broad-shouldered, clad in well-worn, hard-wearing work clothes – a collarless brushed cotton shirt, brown wool trousers, a waistcoat and a tweed jacket.

'So what's happened to you two, walking to the middle of nowhere in the rain?' he asked. His voice was gruff but kindly.

'We were looking for Fields Farm. We must have taken the wrong road,' Esterin replied.

'You've certainly taken the long way round. Hop in.'

The farmer drove off as Esterin slammed the door shut. He headed the way we had come, but took a turning off the road about a mile further, and drove us up into the forested mountains.

'I'm Jemeth Whitley,' he said. 'And you must be Eston and Yenner, my new tenants.'

My heart fell to hear that surname. Perhaps there were lots of Whitleys in the mountains, I rationalised, but could not convince myself.

'It's good to meet you, Jemeth,' Esterin replied. 'Thank you for giving us this chance.'

'It'll be no picnic in the park, I can promise you. You're only here because I can't do it all myself now.'

He explained our duties as his tenants: farming his fields, learning his skills, and taking messages over the mountains, some of which I would need to translate before we passed them on. I wondered why some messages needed to be translated but did not ask, trusting all would soon become clear. The truck rattled and bumped along the cinder tracks as the men discussed the work.

We arrived at Jemeth's farmstead that evening. It was a mixed farm with some arable land and some hillside grazing rights. Jemeth lived in the main farmhouse, a rugged stone building to one side of a collection of outbuildings around a cobble yard. He gave us a labourer's cottage with its own little garden, standing by a mountain stream a field away from the main farm. Before we ate supper together, he took us round his livestock to show us his evening routine. We were up with the dawn next day to join him in the farm's morning routine. The heavier work became ours as soon as we were physically able to cope with it.

Essie and I had both been city dwellers all our lives: our muscles weren't used to hard physical work. But we set to with a will and soon became leaner and fitter. Jemeth never asked about our pasts, so I gradually forgot my fears of being found out as I embraced the tough routine of physical labour. We worked in the fields during the day. In the evening, I translated a bit more of the holy book or sat by the fire knitting – a new skill taught me by an old villager known as Grandma Dora. Occasionally, I had to translate messages for Essie to take over the mountains or to our team leader. These coded messages took priority over the general traffic of gifts and letters from separated family members. The people I was helping to keep in touch were international agents of The Network.

There was no television signal in the hills, so we lost track of what was going on in the rest of the world. Two cats adopted us and Essie got a sheep dog. We loved our new life together and never wanted it to change.

3:7

Autumn turned to winter. As winter gave way to spring, I fell pregnant. And that's when things started to go wrong again.

Our village doctor sent me to the cottage hospital for antenatal classes and additional support, as I was quite old to be a new mother. The midwife was a lovely woman but fully compliant with legislation.

'You village girls, with your unplanned pregnancies!' she said to our class with a fond tut. 'Don't any of you apply for permission before you start?'

'You try saying that to the bull!' said the wag of the class.

'I know, girls: the city's a different world to the farm. But it means I will have another eleven new expectant mothers to register on the system. They'll be coming to tell us off again.'

'Can't you just pretend we don't exist?' asked the woman beside me.

'You know I can't do that. They would send us all to prison. And there'd be no more midwife here in the valley.'

So my baby grew in my womb, and I wished I could have lived anywhere except the Motherland.

One stormy autumn night about a year after we first came, Esterin left with his dog to take a message I had translated over the mountain to the pick-up point, a journey he had made many times. I sat by the fire, knitting a shawl while I waited for him. Because my baby had passed the due date, Jemeth sat with me in the little cottage. He saw the shawl growing on my knitting needles and wiped a tear from the corner of his left eye.

'You remind me so much of my wife, Emmy, Yenner. Your face, the way you sit, the shawl you are knitting. It's so like the shawl she sent to our daughter.'

'How did you find out where your daughter was?' I asked.

'We were so proud of our daughter, being selected for the Government School because of her linguistic skills. She could already speak two languages before she was little more than a baby. The Network helped us follow her career. I told Emmy not to send her that shawl. But she said 'blood is thicker than water' and sent it anyway.'

A charged silence built up between us. While this gruff but kindly farmer struggled to hold back his grief, I fought with guilt and remorse, and the shock of hearing Jemeth himself confirm he was my father. Sister Sontell may have been able to change my identity, but she had had no solution for the conscience I had found. Untrained in matters of the heart and emotions, I had no idea how to handle the dilemma ruining my peace.

'Jemeth, I have something to tell you,' I said but could not go on.

He looked across at me with eyes that seemed to know what I was struggling to say. We sat in silence for some moments, while the fire crackled and burned in the grate, and an occasional back-draft from the storm outside forced a puff of smoke into the room. At length, when I could leave it unsaid no more, I left my knitting in my lap and spoke on.

'Jemeth, the baby I am carrying is your grandchild.'

He nodded and put his paw of a hand over my right hand, where it lay on the arm of my chair.

'I know.' His voice was so quiet I could barely hear it over the sound of the fire and the wind outside.

'I've been wanting to talk to you about all this for so long. I am so sorry. The longer I carry this child, the more I realise how cruel I had been to the woman who bore me, to your Emmy. I don't know how you could bear to face me, knowing what I'd done.'

He sighed and turned away to put another log on the fire.

'The fault is not all yours, Yenner. You cannot help your upbringing. Most of the fault lies with the Motherland – this noble Motherland we fought for and constructed at the end of that disastrous war. We saw our country change, from a land run for the people to a people run for the land. In our own quiet way, we tried to fight against the rot, until it became too much for us.'

'But that's why Essie and I are here, to help you carry on that fight. We love the chance you have given us. Thank you for giving me a second chance.'

Paws scratched at the front door, disturbing us. It was the familiar sound of Essie's dog, Beattie, trying to get in. I leapt up in joy at their return, but when I opened the door, only Beattie entered. She was wet through and limping, with rain-washed blood on her left haunch.

'Something's gone wrong! I must go find Essie!' I said and reached for my coat.

'No! It's too dangerous for you and the child. I'll go,' Jemeth ordered. He picked up his overcoat. I caught his arm.

'No! You can't go up there now! What would I do if something happened to you, too?'

'Don't fret. I'm only away to Jael's to ask one of the boys to go.'

He walked out into the dark stormy night.

Jael's was the local inn and supply depot, where for legal reasons the drinking went on in a back bar known as The Meeting Room. Though we rarely frequented Jael's, Jemeth was well respected there and soon returned after finding help.

'The lads from Upper Stile Farm have gone. They used to do the run before you and Eston.'

He made us more tea. We sat in supportive silence, disturbed only by the crackling flames in the hearth and the click of my knitting needles.

The dogs set off barking in the byre in the early hours of next morning. A few moments later, the lads from Upper Stile Farm pushed open the front door. My Essie hung draped between their shoulders. His face was pale grey, and blood stained the front of his clothes. The lads laid him down on the kitchen table.

I cradled his head in my hands. His eyes flickered open.

'Daizie, I just had to see you one last time,' he gasped.

'What happened?' I asked.

Blood frothed from his mouth. The lads from Upper Stile Farm answered for him.

'The border patrols were trigger-happy tonight.'

'They shot your Eston and his Sidionite contact.'

Essie's head slumped back and his body was no longer responsive. I screamed at him not to go. Then severe pains cramped my swollen stomach. I cradled my belly, panting for breath, and fell to the floor as I blacked out.

I woke in a hospital bed. My body felt wrong. I rubbed my belly and found it was flat again.

'Where's my baby!' I shouted.

The midwife came to my bedside and placed a cool hand on my forehead.

'Welcome back, Yenner. You had us quite worried for a while.'

'But where's my baby?'

'I'm sorry. We couldn't save your son. If Jemeth hadn't brought you here so quickly, we would have lost you too.'

'Can I see him? Please! Just one time…'

They brought in the cold but perfectly formed little body, wrapped in a towel wound high enough to try to hide where the umbilical cord had wrapped around his neck and strangled him. I crushed him to myself, sobbing uncontrollably as I named him Estevan.

In one night, I had lost the two people I held most dear. Not knowing how to cope with the emotions going through me, I wailed in a grief so visceral a nurse gave me a sedative to take me out of the pain.

3:8

After that, Jemeth was very gentle with me. He got me to move from the cottage to the farmhouse and tried to cut back on my duties. But I preferred to work. It took my mind off all I had lost. I became the courier as well as the translator. Fighting the elements to visit the different mountain rendezvous points suited my mood.

A quirk of geography had placed Jemeth's farm in just the right place for the work. In that region, the hill farms still held the farming rights to the hillsides where they stood. Jemeth's farm had not been the only one to be cut in half by the arbitrary borders drawn up in the Treaty of the

Alliance. But it was on the most direct route from Aledion to Cierte in the borderland of Sidion, via the Aledion Pass. The pass was guarded by trigger-happy troops, but they usually patrolled on the west side of the mountain. We took the supposedly impassable route over the east side of the mountain. The authorities could do little about a shepherd looking for lost sheep, no matter how many mountains from home they found him searching. As Jemeth used to say, 'Farming is too basic for politicians to play games with – without us farmers, the whole world would die.'

A lot of the messages I brought home from these arduous journeys now all seemed nonsense. The Network had changed the code base after Essie's death, making the messages strings of unconnected words. The vocabulary was so basic, even a beginner could have translated them.

For safety reasons, I was not told who the team leader was. Jemeth took my translations to him or her and brought their messages back for me to translate and take to the drop boxes in the mountains. Over time, I realised that if a message included the word *frank*, I would take the reply to the Bai Crag drop box. *Apple* referred to the High Moss scree drop box, and *stone* to the Bield Side drop box.

As winter set in, Jemeth showed me how to plan the farm's planting and management for the year. Where before he had treated Essie and me as labourers, now he let me work with him as his daughter. He showed me his planners from all his previous years on the farm, each detail noted down meticulously in his childlike handwriting.

And then one day, he too disappeared.

I was out muck-spreading in the home field when a big grey van drove into the farmyard. Six Youth Police officers leapt out, distinctive in their grey uniforms. They overran the farmyard and the house. Soon they dragged Jemeth out of a byre to throw him into the back of their van.

Jemeth had ordered me not to stop work if that happened, to give no hint of rebellion, to make sure they did not take me too. I felt so helpless. I wanted to go and save him, but he had always told me not to risk myself too if they came for him. So I drove the tractor and the muck spreader with my head down, watching the van out of the side of my eyes until it drove off and disappeared along the farm track.

I came home to the empty farmhouse at teatime to find the fire had gone out and Jemeth's dog whining at the kitchen door to be let in. I milked the cows and bedded them down for the night, fed the chickens and relit the fire. After snatching a bite of bread and cheese, I went down to Jael's to see if anyone there knew what had happened. The faces in The Meeting Room were disconsolate.

'The grey kites have taken Jemeth,' I said at the bar. *Grey kites* was the local term for the Youth Police.

Jael shook his head. Even he looked discouraged.

'He's not the only one. Grandma Dora wants you to call by. When you can.'

I left at once, the door slamming behind me, and crossed the street to a homely cottage, five doors along from the inn.

Grandma Dora was the woman who had taught me how to knit. She had survived long enough to become the village matriarch, respected by all and often called on to resolve disputes. She looked as old as the village itself, short, wiry, bent with age, but with a keen bright eye and a mind as sharp as the blade on my sickle.

She welcomed me into her kitchen. We sat on either side of her table, cradling mugs of tea.

'Hard times have come to our village, Yenner. Fifteen of our menfolk have been arrested, including your Jemeth and the lads from Upper Stile Farm. Those of us who are left must take over their roles, the way you took over Eston's. I am now our team leader. From now on, you will report to me.'

'Was this my doing, too?' I asked, still shouldering the guilt for what I had done to Emmy.

Her mouth stretched into a sad half-smile as she shook her head.

'No, Yenner. We don't yet know who it was, but we know it was not you.'

'Why did they take him and not me?'

'We're not sure. We think a traitor gave the Youth Police a list of names connected with The Network here. The truth will out eventually: we will find out who betrayed us. In the meantime, try to keep going: keep doing what you do. I will help you all I can.'

3:9

So I found myself doing the work of three, often burning the candle at both ends: taking messages across the mountain at night while running the farm all day. Exhausting, but somehow I pushed myself to get through all that needed to be done. And it helped me cope with my grief for the two men I had loved and lost so violently.

Then one day, everything went wrong. The bull got out, the tractor broke down, and I burned my dinner, almost setting fire to the house. I shouted at the dog, smashed a plate and threw the frying pan at the hens. I had no idea how to handle my emotions. I needed to escape.

Then I remembered the wonderful feeling which had spread through my body and mind that day four years before, when Bee had spiked my tea with sedetal. Instantly, the memory caused my body to ache for another taste of that heaven, that amazing feeling of oneness with all creation and the overpowering beauty of the world. A tempting voice in my head said that could all be mine again. All I had to do was go down the hill and call in at Jael's.

I rushed through the rest of the day's chores, buoyed up by the thought of that little measure of heaven later that day. I had seen how the no-hopers did it, the ghostly huddle of broken men in the back corner of The Meeting Room. It was easy enough to do the same.

When I said the magic word, Jael gave me an old-fashioned look of disapproval. I sat down with my tea and my shot at the back of The Meeting

Room, a little apart from the ghostly huddle in the corner. After savouring the prospect for a few seconds, I drained the shot in one go. Then I sat back to wait for that amazing feeling of peace and joy, that wonderful taste of heaven.

It didn't happen. Though the sedetal altered how I felt, it never took me back to the amazing experience of that first high. Instead, it just relaxed me and made me smile. For a while, nothing mattered any more. Time became immaterial. I felt the trade-off was enough.

When I went to Jael's for my fourth measure, a couple of weeks later, he took me through to the storeroom, with the odd excuse that the flour I had ordered had come in.

'But I don't need any. I still have a quarter sack left,' I replied.

'What do you do on that farm? Live on air?'

'No, I live on our produce.'

Jael closed the door behind us, shutting out the people in the bar. His voice dropped, and he looked sideways at me with a suggestive grin.

'I heard you're on the east Whitley mountain run now.'

'Yes, I do all Jemeth and Essie's work now they're gone.'

'On your next trip, how about taking this along too?'

He handed me a sealed envelope.

'What's in it?' I asked.

'Just an order for a few things I can get more cheaply from Sidion than here. Something that mustn't get lost.'

'How did you manage before?'

'I had my own border courier. But they arrested him with Jemeth and the others. I've had a devil of a job sourcing the goods since. You could save me a lot of trouble.'

'What's it worth?'

'You'll get your measure for free.'

I knew he was talking about sedetal, not flour. As the drug had already got its claws in me, I could not refuse.

'Where do I go?' I asked.

'Give it to your usual Sidionite courier. If he doesn't turn up, leave it in Redcliff Cleft. Swap it for the parcel you'll find hidden under the overhang.'

I nodded and slipped the envelope away in an inside pocket. Jael paid me on account that night. He didn't charge me for the shot, just for the tea.

My next trip to the south side of the mountain came round all too soon. I set off on foot an hour before sunset with the sheepdogs by my side and two envelopes hidden in my clothing. Crook in hand, I trudged through the snow, a patient shepherd ranging out across the mountain in search of lost sheep. As I descended the south-east face of the mountain, an Anoether soldier strode across no-man's land to intercept me.

'Good evening, comrade. What business brings you south of the border?' he demanded.

'Looking for two sheep, comrade. Six of my sheep broke out of their paddock last night. I've only found four of them so far.'

'Which farm are you from? Show me your bracelet.'

'Whitley,' I said, taking off a gauntlet-like leather glove to show him my left wrist. He checked the identity bracelet and nodded to let me put the glove back on.

'Good luck with your search. Don't stay out too long if you want to make it back before nightfall. The wolves are hungry tonight.'

'Thank you for your advice, comrade.'

I whistled a search command to the dogs. They obediently ran back and forth, combing the hillside with their noses skimming the snowy ground. The soldier watched them for a few moments while I trudged off. Then he walked away towards the pass on the west side of Whitley mountain.

About twenty minutes later, a Sidionite shepherd trudged into view over the brow of the hill. He shouted at the soldier and walked towards him. They met up near the valley bottom.

'What are you doing in Sidion, soldier? You surely won't be looking for sheep!'

'I'm on patrol, stopping illegal migrants entering Anoeth.'

'This is Sidion, not Anoeth. A soldier found in enemy territory directly infringes the Treaty of the Alliance. Any native finding an enemy soldier on the wrong side of the border can defend his country as he sees fit.'

'This is no-man's land! You shepherds cross it every day.'

'So do our sheep. Your armaments don't. I order you to leave.'

'And if I don't?'

'You'll leave all the faster.'

The soldier stared at him as if weighing up the odds. Then he turned and walked away towards me. When he had covered fifty feet, the Sidionite pulled out a gun and shot him in the back. After checking he was dead, the shepherd strode on up the snowy hillside towards me. My eyes must have shown my horror through the small gap between my hat and my scarf, as he spoke to reassure me when we met. I recognised him as Enn, the Sidionite courier who had always met me since I had taken over the run.

'The snow tonight will bury him before he's missed if the wolves don't find him first. Right, where are you going, if that isn't too dumb a question after I shot your comrade?'

'I'm off to Eleter to see the palace, of course. The best weather for it,' I replied, completing my side of the password exchange.

'Glad to meet you, friend. I'm going there myself,' he said, completing his.

I asked him why he had shot the soldier in the back. He gave a bitter laugh.

'That's the bastard who shot your predecessor in the back and tried to do the same to my sidekick. I recognised his voice.'

A strange mixture of emotions washed through me. I felt appalled at the courier's lack of respect for life, yet overjoyed that Essie's death had been avenged. When I tried to thank him, he just shrugged it off.

'It's dog eat dog out here. What have you got for me?

'Your usual envelope, and an order from Jael Losser.'

We exchanged my two envelopes for his envelope and a small package.

'Hasn't Jael finished building that bloody transmitter yet? More practically, are you armed? From the look on your face, I thought not. Take the soldier's gun in case the wolves turn up before you get home. I don't want yet another replacement just when I've got used to you. See you in three days.'

He turned and walked off into the dusk. I did as he said and took the dead soldier's weapons. Then I returned home through the gathering dark.

3:10

I translated the new message as soon as I got back. It was as cryptic as always. *Apples and pears, Shistinev sea stables, ready page fireworks, Eleter carpet Rabat, black fountain rose, saints versus sinners, four crown days.*

The colour told me it was urgent. I put my coat back on and drove down to the village, parking at Jael's, with the coded message burning in my pocket. Soon I was sitting at Grandma Dora's kitchen table with my hands cupped round a hot mug of tea, while she read and reread the original message and my translation. Her face had paled and her knuckles were white when they gripped the edge of the table.

'Yenner, go to Jael's and send Rosheem to me. Then come straight back here. Quickly! Quickly!'

I threw my coat back on and ran across to Jael's tea room. Rosheem was in the back kitchen, fast asleep with a drunken grin across his face.

'Jael! This is no good! Grandma Dora needs him, now!'

'Can't it wait until the morning?' Jael asked, walking away from me to serve a customer in the bar.

'No, it can't! The message I brought back is vital. She's asked him to come at once.'

Jael spun back to face me with a scowl. 'Then she will get him!'

He slapped the sleeping drunkard hard across the face and threw some cold water over his head. Rosheem stumbled up from his chair with flailing arms and clenched fists. Jael caught his raised hands.

'Rosheem! Go to Grandma Dora's! Now! At once!'

His urgency gave the drunk some focus. Rosheem staggered out of the tearoom without even taking his coat.

Jael turned back to me with a smile, as if nothing had happened.

'Did you collect my delivery, then?'

I handed him the small parcel. He checked its contents and stowed it away in a cupboard, not hearing me as I told him about the trouble I had to get it. When he turned back, he looked at my face.

'You look like you need a drink.'

He poured me a glass of his home-brewed selda in the Meeting Room. It wasn't what I wanted. I was already craving sedetal. I was about to ask for some when a man from the ghostly huddle of no-hope addicts crowded my table. He towered above me, a white-faced zombie homing in on his new victim.

'Who are you?' he demanded, jabbing an emaciated finger at me. 'Eston called you Daizie, when he was dying – the lads said from Upper Stile Farm. You're not Yenner Devlin, are you!'

'No, she isn't,' said another, looming beside him, his face a mask of contempt. 'Since you came here, all we've had is bad luck. You're a Motherland spy!'

'No, I'm just a courier, trying to do a job I wasn't born to. I came here from Govensh, after disappearing over a year ago. The Network sent me here to help when Jemeth couldn't cope any more on his own.'

A third zombie joined them, unfolding a tattered newspaper clipping. He ironed it out on my table with shaking hands.

'I thought I knew your face. Daizin Keberin, the daughter who betrayed her own mother, our dear Emmy Whitley! You're the rat! You're the spy!'

The blood drained from my face as I saw the tattered newsprint photo of my former self. I downed the glass of selda in one and stood up to face my accusers. The crowd in the tea room gathered behind me to block my escape. A scowling farmer stepped forward, his shoulders hunched.

'I think you need to tell us all a little tale. Make it the truth this time. Or you'll wish the wolf pack got you first.'

I raised my head in defiance. He hit out across my chin and sent me sprawling across the floor. I spun round back onto my feet and belted him in the mouth. He staggered back into a friend's arms, caught out by my swift reaction. The friend shoved him forward, back towards me. I pressed back against the wall, preparing for the worst.

'Stop,' Jael ordered. 'No violence. Unless you want us ALL closed down!'

They surged forward in a mindless mob, accusations flying, whipping themselves into a frenzy. I shrank back, paralysed by fear. When the first man raised his fist, I cried out but heard no sound.

'Desist!' Grandma Dora commanded from the door. Though her voice was reedy and far from firm, everyone heard her over the hubbub.

The man faltered and dropped his fist. The mob stepped back and turned aside. Grandma Dora's adamant face had us shuffling back to our seats, the sheepish men like naughty school children caught in the act. She marched into the centre of the room and glowered at the ringleader.

'Are you jealous of Yenner? Or do you turn on her for some other reason?'

'She's not who she says she is. She's the government spy.'

'Yes, she is,' others said, but with less conviction.

'Is she? Then why did Yenner bring back a code black message from the mountain tonight? A message she delivered to me right away so that I could send a courier to try to halt the danger? Our Motherland is about to fire some missiles which could start a new world war. We could all be wiped off the map.'

'It's a hoax,' someone shouted.

'It's not a hoax,' Jael said. 'I've already heard a rumour today about some people quitting the cities for the borders. That would explain it.'

'What's that to us?' asked one of the ghostly huddle.

Grandma Dora looked at him with baleful eyes. 'If our missiles at Shistinev destroy the two foreign capitals, the Sidionite premier will give the order to destroy our country. That would be the end of us. Not just the Motherland. It would destroy what little's left of this tattered remnant of our world. All of us.'

She slumped into a carver chair.

'Recharge the glasses, Jael. Yenner Devlin will now tell you the story of her life. I will know if she lies, and I will say so. And while you listen, Aledionites, remember: I know as much detail about each one of you. Think twice before you act against her again, because I will act against you. None of us are blameless here.'

What could I do? Though I longed for my measure and then my bed, I sat there at my table in The Meeting Room and told my life story. I admitted everything, from betraying Emmy Whitley to becoming Jael's drug courier. While I spoke, the only sound I heard was the passing of jars of home-fermented wine. When I finished, no one else spoke until Grandma Dora broke the silence.

'Thank you, Yenner.' She used the table to help her get to her feet. 'Jael, give her what she wants. I know you have it. And Yenner, I know it will kill you. So did you when you made the bargain.'

She stumbled to the door. I ran to open it for her.

'Thank you, thank you, comrade, for saving my life.'

'Yenner, you should have come straight back to me.'

She slipped out into the night.

Jael handed me a small bottle and told me to leave. Relief washed over me to feel the bottle in my hand. Despite all that had just happened, I felt elated as I drove back to the farmstead. I had got my measure. How excited I felt at the prospect of drinking it back home. And perhaps this time when I took it, I would go beyond the zombie state and taste heaven again, for the second time ever.

If I had been the village villain that day, the hero was Rosheem. He had raced through the mountains on his home-built cross-country motorbike to take the code black message to a Network contact. The contact mobilised other members of the Anoether Network to sabotage the missiles at Shishtinev. We only found out about their mission two days later, when the news channels reported an 'incident' at a security establishment. Three saboteurs had tried to gain access from the air: two had died and one was being held in a secure hospital. The proof of their successful mission came two days after that, when Eleter and Rabat did not get wiped off the map and Anoeth was not destroyed.

Only Grandma Dora respected me for my part in it all. The other villagers just tolerated me. Spring came late that year, but where the farmers helped each other out to get through, they never quite managed to help me. The Whitley farm came through better than some, despite my increasing drug abuse. The only way I could face crossing the mountain by the east screes route was to take a measure of sedetal in the morning to calm the jitters while I worked, to give me courage when I went, and to shut my mind up enough to sleep after I got back.

Then I got word The Network's transmitter was going live soon. They would no longer need me to act as a courier over the mountain. I panicked, thinking that would stop my Sedetal run too. But Jael told me not to worry.

I was sitting in my corner of The Meeting Room one night, depressed because I felt useless and alone, when the door flew open and a worker from Hill End Farm marched in, demanding his bottle. His body was shaking in withdrawal, and beads of sweat ran down his tortured face as cravings gnawed at his vital organs.

'What bottle's that, Hanney?' Jael asked, pouring him a glass of selda.

'You know full well! I've run out. You didn't send it with the order. I must have some.'

Jael scowled. 'Not until you pay me!'

'But I can't pay you! You've got everything I have but the clothes on my back.'

'Then you'll have to do without.'

Hanney lunged at him. Jael stepped aside and let him fall into the laps of the ghostly huddle in the corner. Hanney lumbered to his feet and squared up to Jael.

'If that's the way you want it, Jael!' His voice dropped from a roar to a venomous whisper. 'I'll make you all pay for it like I did last time.'

'What last time?' asked one of the ghostly huddle in the other corner.

We all held our breath. Hanney ranted on, oblivious to our reactions.

'*I want money*, Jael said. *I haven't got any*, I said. *Then get some*, he said. *Like how*, I said. *Like I do*, he said: *a little secret here, a little secret there, every now and then.* So I took his tip. And they gave me money, lots of money. But it's all gone!'

Rosheem grabbed him by the shoulder and spun him round. 'You mean it wasn't Yenner Whitley who betrayed our men?'

Panic crossed Hanney's tortured face as he realised how his insane rant had condemned himself with his own words.

'You will do nothing again!' Rosheem growled.

His paw of a hand went for Hanney's throat. Before his grasp could close, Hanney spun back out of his reach. Hanney ran out through the main door into the square. Rosheem charged after him. The rest of us turned our backs to make sure we saw nothing more.

Rosheem must have caught up with the turncoat a short way down the street. When I went home that night, Hanney's corpse was lying in the gutter. It had gone before the Youth Police could find it the next morning.

3:11

Summer came a month later. The cereal crops sown in the valley were promising a good yield despite the late sowing. I checked Jemeth's farming diaries and sowed two of the lower fields following his crop rotation. But I felt less inclined to work, and being a relative novice at farming, I could tell the Whitley fields did not look as good as the neighbours'. The furrows weren't straight, the germinating seeds looked patchy, and as they grew into oats and wheat, the seedlings lagged behind those in neighbours' fields.

There was little help at sheepshearing time, either. The village shearing team never quite got round to helping me shear my flock. At least no one chased me away when I visited other farms to remind myself of the best techniques before I sheared the Whitley flock myself. I sold the wool in a nearby auction which brought in some much-needed money to pay the ever-rising costs of my habit. I was hurtling towards the state Hanney had ended up in, living to take the drug to take away the shakes and the gnawing feeling inside, and ignoring the need to eat to live.

By late summer, the farm was in a mess. The Whitley harvest fields looked stunted compared to those of the other farms. Each evening when I sat in my corner in The Meeting Room, waiting for my second measure, I fancied I was the butt of murmured jokes.

I was there again one night, when the main door opened and in walked an old man we regulars felt we knew but could not place.

'What has happened? Who is trying to destroy me?' he asked, his lined face charged with pain. We recognised his voice at once, worn and tired though it now sounded after all he had been through.

'Jemeth!' Jael welcomed. 'Have a drink on the house. What happened to you?'

My father was a shadow of his former self. The stout, patient never-say-die farmer I had last seen less than a year before, was now gaunt, emaciated, bent under the weight of oppression, his face sunken and aged. Hardest of all to see, there was no spark of hope in his eyes.

'Just tea, Jael. You don't know how good it is to be here again. I never thought I would make it back. We were betrayed, by Hill End's hand Hanney.'

'We know,' Rosheem said.

'He's dead,' Jael said, and gave him his tea.

Jael moved on to give me a glass of selda and my measure. Jemeth looked at me. Recognition slowly came to him, and as it did, his shoulders slumped further. He picked up his tea and sat down at my table.

'Yenner, my Yenner,' he whispered. He wiped a tear from my cheek. 'What have they done to you, lass? Where's the handsome young woman I left behind?'

'She's on the way out with sedetal,' Jael said.

'Why, my child? What has happened? Where are all your friends?'

'What friends?' I asked. 'I have no friends.'

'But why?'

When I did not answer, he turned to ask the other farmers the same question.

'She's too ashamed to admit it!' said one of the ghostly huddle.

'What?' Jemeth asked.

'She's your daughter!' Rosheem declared. 'Grandma Dora made her tell her story, her true story. How she betrayed her mother, your wife, and half of Aledion with her. The woman you took in under your own roof was the one who almost destroyed you three years back!'

'So you left my daughter, my own flesh and blood, to come to this? Just stood by and watched?'

His eyes searched their faces. One by one, their heads dropped to avoid his gaze. I heard the main door close behind them and presumed someone had left the inn rather than face him.

'Did you think I didn't know that? She told me herself, and I found compassion enough to forgive her. Her confession told me she had finally seen through the Motherland's lies. Did you not see how proud I was that she now chose to fight beside us for the cause?'

He broke down and turned his face away. Grandma Dora pressed through the men by the main door and crossed the room to sit with him. Her aged hand gently touched his shoulder. He looked up into her eyes.

'Welcome back, Jemeth. Yes, your daughter has worked hard for the cause in your absence. And she has run Whitley with little help from the other farmers. Be proud of Yenner, for all she has done despite all her problems.'

Grandma Dora sat at our table and waved to Jael to bring more tea. She asked Jemeth for news of the others arrested the same day as him.

His face was grave as he answered her. 'Your son, the leader, is dead, and so is the treasurer. State Security officers shot our police contacts and tortured our four agents until they spoke or died. Our courier from Oucerne killed himself. The rest were taken off to a mental health facility, and we didn't hear anything of them again. Maxim from Hill End and I were only set free because we didn't have long to live. Maxim collapsed on the way home and died at Entelliard.'

Grandma Dora sighed and stood up to leave. We followed her out into the nighttime street, silvered by the cold light of the full moon. She returned to her cottage. I took Jemeth to the cattle truck parked behind Jael's and helped him climb up into the passenger seat.

'How is the farm?' he asked.

I walked round to the other side and hauled myself into the driving seat. It gave me time to think of what to say. As Jemeth had defended me in front of the village, I was honest.

'The buildings and the barns are neglected, the crops will be poor, but the livestock are tolerably well. I spent all the wool money on drink and drugs. So I have failed you.'

'You are not the one who failed me, Yenner.'

I drove us back to the Whitley farm. When we turned down the track to the farmhouse, Jemeth asked me to stop by the cornfield. My heart sank as I brought the truck to a halt and turned off the lights. Our eyes adjusted to the moonlight. He looked out across the field of rippling corn and sighed.

'You did all that, with little help? You've done a fine job for a townie. Even the hedges and fences look good in this light. Why did you paint such a grim picture?'

'Because it is grim, when you look at the Hill End farm.'

'They are seventh generation farmers, and they've got a good team of hands. You're a novice, and you did this on your own.'

His voice sounded stronger, his bearing more upright. As I drove him to the farmhouse, he looked out over his land with a childlike pleasure to be home. He stood beside the farmyard gate, breathing in deep lungfuls of fresh air. Then he walked into the house, and cried in delight to find his slippers where he had left them by the hearth. He took off his boots and sat at the table, caressing its familiarity.

I stirred some life into the fire, made a pot of tea and set out some bread and cheese before him. He ate and drank with joy and gratitude. His response to his homecoming made me ashamed of my own feelings of futility and depression.

'Yenner, perhaps the crops aren't as good as Hill End's. Perhaps our barns do need repairs and the house cleaned. Perhaps we do have no money and we are both ill. But at least we have a home, and a working farm, and each other.'

He paused with a reflective smile and shook his head.

'When I came back, I expected to find you gone and the farm in ruins. I came home to die. But you have given me a reason to live again. Sick though we both may be, we can try to forge a new future from the wreckage of the past, however bleak our present.'

His simple faith in us inspired me to find a little faith too. That night, I cleaned up the hovel I had lived in and made it a home again. The next morning, I began to harvest the corn under Jemeth's instruction. Every day I harvested, he sat by the field gate to watch, his face gilded by the autumnal sunshine. We would eat lunch in the field, him, sitting on a chair I had brought, while I sat on the edge of the stubble. When I said I needed to go to Jael's each lunchtime, he nodded in understanding and sent me off.

It was the last day of harvesting the wheat. I left him sitting in his chair gazing across the reaped field that lunchtime. He was still sitting there when I returned later. He had a contented smile. But when I called to him, he did not turn, and when I stood before him, he did not look up. I touched his hand. It was cold. I felt for a pulse, but there was none.

Jemeth Whitley was dead.

126

3:12

I drove down to Jael's and drank a bottle of selda in The Meeting Room. I drank desperately, intensely, oblivious to the people around. At one point, Rosheem tried to say something to me. At another, Jael offered me some food. A wall of incomprehension shut them out from me.

Then Grandma Dora sat by me and took my hand.

'What's the matter, Yenner, dear?'

I stared at her through clouded eyes, but could not find the words to answer her.

'Is Jemeth all right?'

I shook my head.

'Where is he?'

'In the field I was harvesting, sitting there in the sunlight, dead.'

'He came home to die where his heart lay, Yenner. Don't worry. We'll sort things for you. Stay here for now. You'll be quite safe. I'll come back for you later.'

She left the inn, speaking to Jael on her way out.

My mind churned like a whirlpool, pulling me down into a nightmare with no escape. The lifeline that could have saved me had gone with Jemeth's death. Around me, voices echoed condolences beyond that wall of incomprehension. When I looked up at them, they looked like frightening shadows lurking in the depths of a room that had become bent and black.

'Jael?' I called, desperate to break through the trap closing in around me.

'Don't you think you've drunk enough? Here, have some tea.'

I grasped the spectre's solid arm.

'Jael, help me, please! I'm falling into hell! Please, give me something to chase this evil away.'

'I'm sorry, Yenner – I don't have anything. The order didn't come through last night.'

The walls bent around me and the ceiling rippled like the sea as the room folded inwards. I leapt up to find the door before the room crushed me. The floor rose to trip me as the door moved away. Someone tried to help me but I shook them off. Then the door came near again and I stumbled out into the street.

I climbed up into the cattle truck, pushing someone away who was trying to stop me. As the engine started up, the dials danced in front of me and the pedals and levers fought back. I forced it into first gear. It shot forward up the road heading out of town towards the mountains.

I don't know how long I drove or where the truck took me to. The journey stopped when the truck plunged downwards and rolled over. The next thing I knew, it was morning. I found myself in an unknown valley in the mountains, well off the road. My mind crawled with a desperate craving I could not satisfy. A cold emptiness deadened my heart.

I pulled myself out of the wrecked vehicle and began to climb into the scrubland, looking for the road I had driven off. The road never appeared. I reached the crest of the hill and looked out across a vista of unknown mountains and valleys. All was devoid of human habitation. I wondered whether to walk on and die slowly of starvation and exposure, or to end my worthless life by throwing myself from a rock.

A gentle breeze ruffled my hair. In the heart of the breeze echoed a song, an unearthly song I had not heard before. I turned my face to the wind and felt the pain and cravings slip away. Below me spread a strange, almost numinous valley leading to a distant ocean. The valley looked like it was part of a desert, the colour of sand unrelieved by any patch of green. The only feature was a meandering dip where a river may once have run. Yet from the heart of that valley flowed the enchanted song.

I scrambled down the hillside and stumbled across the desert in search of the source of the song. It was a struggle to keep my footing because the ground was covered in bones, human bones.

For a moment, the wind stopped and the song fell silent. The sun beat down without mercy from above. Crows circled, hoping for their next meal. The ominous atmosphere made me try to turn back, but I couldn't. All the hills edging the valley looked the same, so I did not know which one to choose.

A gentle breeze caressed my hair and the enchanting song returned. I turned my face back into the wind and walked on towards its source. As the sun set, my feet brought me to this ruined village. Someone lit a lantern and hung it outside the inn beside the bridge.

I opened the tavern door and came in.

MAGGIE SHAW

Part 4
Astell Irva's Story

4:1

This is not the first time I have stayed here, at the Drysau Bridge Inn.

This time, I looked down on my bleeding body lying there in the dust and cried, 'Not again!' Then I left my body behind to walk away into the mountains and found myself back here.

Yes, you can return to life from here, but only if you choose to.

I first came here some four years ago. I was the teenage skipper of a coastal fishing boat then and I had made a lot of unwise choices. The boat became my charge as the oldest of the family when my father died, even though I wasn't male. We had lost Father overboard in a storm and his body washed up some days later, further down the Ouslauv coast. He left behind my mother and five children.

At sixteen, I was the only one in our family besides our mother who was of an age to run a business. It was tough competing with the other fisherfolk. In an industry dominated by men, our child crew struggled to bring home good catches and I rarely got a good price at market. We did little more than exist. Then a man made me an offer I knew was wrong but couldn't turn down. I thought of the hungry faces at home and the way my mother looked old before her time, and I had to accept.

Up in the hills at the back of us, the farmers grew cash crops like opium poppies. They needed boats to take their products along the coast to their customers in Sidion. The money was good, I got a small cut of the produce, and we even got to keep the fish we caught.

My family lived very well for a few years, and I got too dependent on the goods I was shipping. Then my brother Kivvy chose to ruin it all. When he turned sixteen, he became the male head of our household and claimed the family boat as his right. He stopped our drug runs and returned the boat to full-time fishing. I argued with him to change his mind but failed because after our father's death, it had always been his property in law. It felt so unfair, but I was powerless to change how things were done.

The drug cartel was none too pleased. And I was too strung out to deal with the problem. When the cartel claimed I owed them thousands for what I'd used, I ran away and hid in another drug-fuelled trip out. The Shark's heavies caught me leaving a drug den and beat me up. They left me for dead in a squalid back alley, among the rubbish and the shit.

It would have been so easy to die then. No more worries, no more cares. I remember the peace of having no future. But then I landed here at Drysau Bridge and stayed the night at this inn. Three other people told their stories. Somehow, they ignited the tiniest spark of defiance inside me.

At the end of the night, we all walked out into the dawn with the stark choice: the berries or the sea. I watched the others walk over the bones to the shore and stride off into the ocean. The peace on their faces made it so tempting to join them. Struggling with my decision, I wrenched a berry from its stalk and crushed it in my mouth. The juice was bittersweet. Barely had I tasted it when it was gone.

I woke up in a white room, lying between white sheets with my head on a white pillow. Two women wearing white wimples smiled at me.

'Am I in heaven?' I asked.

Pain hit me: wave upon wave from every part of my body. This couldn't have been heaven. But it might have been purgatory.

'You are in the Convent of the Sisters of Clemency,' one said. 'I'm Sister Mercy, and this is Sister Patience.'

'Some thugs gave you a good going over. You are fortunate someone found you before it was too late,' said Sister Patience.

'It doesn't feel very fortunate at the moment,' I croaked.

Tears were leaking from my puffy eyes, but I couldn't move my arms to wipe them away. My limbs were in splints. It hurt to breathe, my face was swollen, and I was missing a tooth. Then the withdrawals came over me. Cold sweat drenched my body, and I became delirious.

My next memory was waking up to the sound of children's voices. They were singing a harvest song. It spoke of reaping what we have sown. I cried again. This time, I had a free hand to wipe away my tears. My body was sore but no longer screamed in pain. Though there were scabs on my face, most of the swelling had gone. I asked for a mirror, but the Sisters wouldn't bring me one for several more days. When I finally saw my reflection, it was easy to see why. I had never been a beauty, and fishing is a tough business, but the bent nose and these scars were something else.

It was a long, slow recovery. The Sisters introduced me to their cycle of work, prayer, confession, and devotion to the Creator of the Universe. Their disciplined way of life taught me the joy that can be found in service. They treated me as someone of worth – I had not known such respect previously, and my opinion of myself was very poor. They helped me work through the issues that had nearly destroyed me. Because they were totally honest with me, I could be totally honest with them.

They also showed me how to pray for others, not just for myself. A couple of months into my recovery, we had heard news of the Freedom Marchers Massacre in Govensh, Anoeth. The temple priests and worshippers had been celebrating their traditional New Year festival on the streets of Govensh, when the Anoether Youth Police misinterpreted their Hola Mohalla as the start of a rebellion and fired into the crowd, killing several people who had been taking part in the play fight. The Sisters encouraged me to pray for those who had died, for those who were dependent on them, for those who had murdered them, and for the diplomats and negotiators who were working to bring about reconciliation between Anoeth and Ouslau. It was the first time I had engaged with the idea of praying blessings on our enemies, and I found it very hard to do.

The Sisters were so lovely and supportive of me despite my struggles, I wanted to stay with them for ever. But they wouldn't let me. It was because I had come back from Drysau Bridge. They showed me the legend in one of their holy books.

There is a valley in the mountains that cannot be found by those who seek it, but reveals itself to those who do not. The valley is littered with the bones of those who died in battle, and the river flowing through it is red with the blood of martyrs. A day will come when the peace the world seeks will cover the earth, and nation will live in accord with nation. And the river will fall dry. But then men will return to their old ways and the waters will feed the vine once more. And those who eat the berry will return with news of Drysau Bridge.

'You have come back from Drysau Bridge, Astell. Thus we know you have a different path to tread,' the Abbess explained. 'Take heart, for we will always be here to help you when you need us.'

I wept, because I wanted to stay in the safety of their harbour. But that is not the purpose of a boat.

4:2

As part of my recovery, the Sisters wanted me to work, to occupy my mind and my days. A return to the family business was out of the question with drug lords likely to finish the job they had failed to do before. Instead, the Sisters sent me to serve in the chapel at Anva, the next port along the coast. Like the chapel at Irva, this small house of worship struggled to pay its way, and I worked for just bed and board. The chapel needed extensive repairs but could not afford the labour. It also had a storehouse it had turned into a café, and was doing wonderful work among the down-and-outs attracted to the port.

My job there was to beg local residents and businesses for materials to repair the walls and dome and for paint to cover over the repairs. Whatever I got in donations was used to keep the building standing. In the evenings,

I served in the café, helping vagrants and the destitute find food and shelter. I got into many a conversation there about how the Sisters of Clemency had restored me to health, to sanity and to usefulness. Indeed, the conversations often interfered with my duties. I would hastily break off when the café manager came near. After the fourth such interruption, he took me to one side.

We were in the larder, surrounded by empty shelving and two depleted sacks of flour. I hung my head and looked at the floor in my shame that my boss had caught me yet again.

'Astell, look at me,' he said. His voice was gentle, persuasive rather than commanding.

I looked up into his face and caught sight of the friendly smile crinkling his eyes before I dropped my head again.

'Astell, never think it is wrong to talk to the people who come here. They come in off the streets where all they've heard are insults, threats and orders to move on. Yours may be the first friendly voice they've heard in a long, long time. Yes, give them what they need – food, clothes and shelter – whatever we have, but never stop honouring them with your respect.'

From then on, my role at the chapel changed. I spent less time begging and more time working in the café. Its opening hours were extended and support groups met there. I often spoke about my miraculous recovery from dying drug addict to a life transformed. Other people heard my message and turned their lives around as I had done. The chapel did so much good, yet it faced a constant financial struggle to survive.

News of the chapel's success in reducing homelessness, destitution and active addiction reached the religious authorities in Rabat the following year. They wanted me to move to our capital and do the same thing there. I didn't want to go.

'This is where I belong,' I told my supervisor. 'By the sea, working with people like the people I grew up among, in the sort of place I understand. And I would be letting you down and the chapel if I went.'

The manager shook his head and gave me another of those friendly smiles which crinkled his eyes.

'Astell, you would not let us down by leaving us now. Thanks to you, we already have several volunteers to take your place. Go with our blessing. Transform the lives of the poor in Rabat the way you've changed so many lives here.'

4:3

The request from the religious authorities did not include money for travel. I had to walk there, every last mile, with my few possessions in a bag on my back, including the precious letters of introduction provided by the chapel and the Sisters of Clemency. It gave me a lot of time to think.

I had never realised how big Ouslau is; how much of it is desert and how much of the rest is the poorest of farming lands. Maybe I hadn't listened to lessons in school as a child, for it surprised me to see how relatively well-off we had been in Irva, living in a port. Even when we had no money, we could always catch fish for a meal and shelter in the stone houses from the winter storms raging outside.

The biggest town on my journey, Sangha, was another revelation to me. I saw how the wealth of that town was as much greater than Irva's as Irva's was greater than the poverty of the desert villages. People stared at me in the streets, crossing to the other side of the road to avoid the dusty tramp. I found the town's main place of worship with relative ease as it towered above the rest of the buildings. It was a temple rather than a chapel, and its holy leader was reluctant to see me until I showed his acolyte my letter of introduction from the Sisters of Clemency. Then the temple staff treated me with the greatest courtesy, providing a change of clothes, introducing me to the volunteers preparing food in the kitchens below the place of worship, and seating me with the temple dignitaries at the communal meal which was served daily in the temple complex.

It was there I met the young woman who was to become my travelling companion for the rest of my journey and my good friend. The temple Granthi brought her over to sit with me.

'Esteemed guest Astell, this is Fayell, our outreach worker. Fayell has also been invited to work with the lost in Rabat. You will have much in common.'

Fayell was a lean colt of a woman with short hair. She dressed like a youth in a sand-coloured tunic and trousers, unlike the traditional long colourful robes and uncut hair of the women in the temple. Her impish smile won me over right away. We started talking as if we had always been friends, comparing our backgrounds and our faith in a spirit of cooperation and learning. She was a child of dirt farmers who had fallen into the wrong company in her teens, and had also been rescued by her faith.

'We must speak with the Lore Keeper before we go, Astell,' she said. 'He is a Jathedar, and he wishes to speak with us before we go to the big city.'

We met the Lore Keeper three days later, the day before we set out on the next stage of our journey to Rabat. He met us in the temple library, an old man seated among the books, his beard untrimmed, his hair wound out of sight in a turban.

'Welcome, my children. Be seated and take tea with me,' he said. His voice was clear and firm despite the great age suggested by his stooped posture and wrinkled skin.

We bowed and sat where he indicated, on cushioned couches around a low carved-wood table. An attendant poured tea for us in dainty blue and white china bowls. I watched how the Lore Keeper supped from his bowl before trying to drink the tea myself. He held his bowl between the thumb and middle finger of his left hand and sipped gently. Fayell handled her bowl of tea with similar ease, but I spilt some on my first attempt. When I went to wipe up the spill with my sleeve, an attendant patted it dry for me. The Lore Keeper ignored my clumsiness.

'There is much for you both to do in Rabat, and as we commission you to go, know that our prayers will continue to support you in your work. Astell Irva, you come from a place of the Books and the Star, but you come to us from a temple of the Book and the Cross. Fayell Orla, you came here from a place of The Wheel. And we meet here, at the place of the Book and the Scimitar. In this room, we represent, in a small way, our country as it now stands – a land that shelters all faiths who hold the Supreme Being at their heart.'

Though I didn't fully understand what he meant, his words made me reflect about the different houses of worship I had come across in my travels. I saw that though people worshipped in different ways, they all worshipped the same All-Powerful God, whatever the name they used to address that God. The Lore Keeper gave me time to process what I was thinking before he continued.

'Once, all our island continent followed the Wheel. That was before the War of Destruction. Nine-tenths of the world was destroyed in the clash caused by tyranny and greed. When the refugees flooded our shores, we took them all in – there was nowhere else for them to go. We respected their common humanity.'

He sighed and shook his head.

'That was something they did not respect. They demanded lands to live where they could support themselves. We agreed to that. But our leaders were not wise to their ways. Though we still have more land than they do, our country now has the poorest lands. The refugees used the Treaty of the Alliance to take control of the best.'

'How did they manage to do that?' Fayell asked, astonished.

'Our leaders forgot the need to be cunning as serpents when they were being innocent as doves. We had no self-serving agenda, whereas the people in need had. The negotiations were long and challenging. What seemed like gains for Ouslau at the end of the process proved to be less valuable than they looked on paper.'

'What does this have to do with us going to Rabat tomorrow?' I asked.

He shook his head in response to my impatience.

'One of the terms we wanted in the Treaty of the Alliance, was for all people of the three Father books to live in Sidion with the rich warmongers. Their misinterpretation of their scriptures had spawned their belief in subjugating creation, and their empire-building had helped cause the War of Destruction. The Sidionite politicians refused that clause. As a result, only agnostics joined the capitalists in Sidion. Most of the atheists joined the socialists in Anoeth, and most people of faith brought their faiths to Ouslau, joining the people of The Wheel who were already here.'

'I still don't understand,' I said, frowning.

'Rabat will open your eyes if you have the eyes to see. When you do understand the consequences, come back here and I will explain more.'

4:4

Fayell and I arrived in Rabat three weeks later. She went to live and work in a unit in the suburb of Chana, supporting people who struggled with mental illness. I joined the addiction rehabilitation centre in nearby Saunda. Our paths often crossed, and we both drew strength from our friendship. Whenever we could, we spent our time off together.

Rabat is a city of the wealthy and the beautiful: sumptuous mansions, luxury cars, attractive people. At first, I did not notice the absence of the poor and people with disabilities or deformities in the heart of the capital, until Fayell and I started exploring the famous buildings on foot. As we walked together along the streets, people would avert their eyes or cross to the other side to avoid us. They expected us to hide away in our suburban ghettos or return to the provinces, out of sight and out of mind. This upset Fayell more than me because she had not experienced such attitudes before. It had often happened to me because of the scars on my face.

At the heart of Rabat is the elegant National Garden of Worship. Ouslau's twelve national temples of worship stand there in a massive circle around the edge of the garden. Our seat of government, the Assembly House, stands in the centre. The thirteen buildings are palatial in their size and their design. They have white marble walls and polished bronze roofs which reflect the sunlight and dazzle the eyes. A symbolic golden finial tops each temple, showing the faith practised there.

Despite the peaceful atmosphere in the gardens, the eight radial roads through them were busy with traffic travelling between the buildings. Everywhere we looked, gardeners worked to keep the lawns and flowerbeds in perfect order. We sat on a bench by a fountain and watched cascades of water spouting from the mouths of three white marble fish to land in the pink marble bowl below. The splashing water sounded so restful, I could have stayed there for hours. That bench became our special place.

The next time we met there, we visited the temple nearest to our seat. I thought we might not be let in, but Fayell was confident we would.

'They are public buildings, so we should be able to look inside,' she said.

The temple we visited was topped with the golden symbol of The Wheel. Around the building's stepped base fluttered bunting made from colourful prayer-flags. We ascended the steps to the massive oak entrance doors. They stood open in welcome. Inside the huge dark dome, we saw people meditating on mats scattered across the patterned mosaic floor. Somewhere above sounded a deep, resonant bell. Several people got up to leave and returned their mats to an usher on their way out. The usher invited us to collect a mat and take their places to meditate. We set our mats down in a darker corner and copied the actions of the people near us. Their manner of worshipful meditation was not a part of our own traditions. I struggled to sit still and was glad to leave with others when the bell rang again.

As we left the temple, an old woman invited us to place a donation in a box labelled for the upkeep of the building.

'We have no money. We don't get paid for the work we do,' Fayell said.

'Then may enlightenment be a blessing to you both,' the woman said, with a warmth that made us want to go back again.

On our next visit to the garden, we went to see the temple with the crescent moon on the roof. The ushers received us with courtesy when we walked in through their main doors. They provided us with shawls to cover our heads, and directed us up some stairs to a carpeted chamber overlooking the main worship hall. There, a young woman explained to us in a low voice what was happening in the main hall below while we observed it through a lattice-panelled wall. Rows of men knelt in prayer on the floor and then sat where they had knelt to listen to a sermon given by their worship leader.

'Where are the rest of the women?' Fayell asked, looking behind us at the eight other women also in the room.

'Women are permitted to worship at home when their duties require that. They do not have to come here to pray,' the young woman replied.

We listened to the sermon, which was preached in our own language and concerned the virtues required to live a good life: kindness, charity, forgiveness, honesty, patience, justice, respect for the elders, keeping one's word and self-control. These were virtues we both aspired to and gave us much to talk about when we went back to our separate homes later that afternoon.

On another visit, we went to see the temple with the cross on the roof. A tall portico of marble columns provided a shelter outside the three main doors of heavily studded oak. We ascended the steps and tried each of the doors in turn. All three were locked. Then Fayell noticed a sign directing us to the side of the building where a small door led us into a shop. We entered and looked at all the goods on display: books, prayer cards, candles and beads, none of which we could afford. An assistant noticed our bewildered faces and stopped stacking shelves to speak to us.

'You can get a ticket to enter at the cash desk,' she said, pointing to the till.

'Is it free to go in?' Fayell asked.

'No, it's ten rials. This building does cost a lot to run.'

'We have no money. We don't get paid for the work we do,' I said.

'Ah, you come as pilgrims. Just show your shell at the cash desk and your entry is free.'

'We have no shells. We have not come from the coast,' Fayell said.

'No problem: we have pilgrim shells for sale at the cash desk.'

'And how much are they?' I asked.

'Seven rials.'

We shook our heads and walked back out.

4:5

The suburb of Saunda is a place of great poverty hidden away in the dirty back streets behind one of the main routes into the city from the coast. I worked in the addiction rehabilitation centre, which was based in a near-derelict hall attached to a small chapel practising the faith of the book and the cross. The prefabricated kit building had poor insulation, which made it costly to heat or keep cool. One priest ran the complex with the help of a deacon as his support worker. Both worked tirelessly for little reward.

I walked into their lives during a heated argument between them about money and expenses. They both looked up, startled, when I opened their office door.

'Come back tonight. The support group doesn't start for two hours,' the deacon ordered. She was a short stocky woman dressed in black cast-offs, with a broad, tired face.

'Thank you, I will. But you may want me to stay. According to this letter, you've been expecting me.'

I handed her the letters of introduction with the original order from the authorities to go there on top. She snatched the papers from my hand and glanced through them, passing each one to the priest as she finished it. Her face flushed.

'Astell Irva, 'I am so sorry for being so rude when you have walked all this way to join us. This is our priest, Father Janus, and I am Deacon Dymphna.'

Father Janus put down my papers and shook my hand. He was tall and scrawny and looked old before his time, but his handshake was confident and firm. The clothes he wore had been made for a person three inches shorter, their colour washed out to a patchy beige with frequent laundering. Yet a power radiated from him which convinced me, even before he spoke, that he was a person of true faith and worthy of my trust.

'At last, Astell. We feared you were never coming. You don't know how much your help will mean to us here.'

He handed back the letters of introduction, instructed Dymphna to put away the accounts for the night, and took me through to the kitchen for something to eat and drink. Dymphna joined us a few moments later. We spent the whole of the two hours before the support group meeting talking about the church and its outreach, my practical skills and experience working with the poor and marginalised, and how they hoped my work there would help them.

There was a lot of work for me to do there. The buildings were in poor repair, but many of their faults were easily remedied by someone with practical skills. I spent my first couple of weeks mending holes, unblocking drains, repairing the roofs and tightening the joints on squeaking chairs. I cleaned the kitchen ovens properly, which got them working better. And, after a few weeks of sleeping on a wood and canvas camp bed I had to put away each morning, I made myself a little bedroom in an old store cupboard by clearing out the contents, repairing anything that could be used and disposing of the rest.

Every evening, I helped Dymphna run the addiction support group. She was a generous and kindly group leader, but I could tell from the way she spoke she had no personal experience of addiction. The first group I attended with her was little more than two hours of grumbles and resentments from the eleven shivering attendees who had only come there for the shelter and the meagre refreshments.

Not wanting to endure another two hours of grumbles and resentments the following night, I spoke first after Dymphna had opened the meeting. I talked about my recovery, how I had used my faith in the Big One Upstairs, God, to overcome the temptation to abuse the drugs available to me, and the importance of practising a daily attitude for gratitude. That last bit was more contentious than I expected, with each attendee in turn listing all the problems which stopped them from being grateful. One was quite insulting about the scars on my face, too, until Dymphna intervened.

'Remember the rules of this group. We don't comment about other members. We only talk about ourselves,' she said. Despite the gentle tone of her voice, the attendee took notice and apologised.

Over time and at least a fortnight's meetings, the atmosphere of the group changed from depressed negativity to a faint perception of hope. People came more regularly and the numbers attending grew in ones and twos.

A month after my arrival, most of the repairs had been done, and I had worked out a simple maintenance schedule to prevent more problems. With a bit of time on my hands, I asked Father Janus if I could start using the hall and kitchen to run a basic recovery café during the day.

'That sounds a wonderful idea,' he said, 'but we simply can't afford it. We don't have enough money to pay for fuel and food.'

'We tried it before,' Dymphna said. 'Lots of people used the service, but we never had enough to go round.'

'At least let me try again!' I said. 'And this time, when you ask for help, try this three-pronged approach: ask God, ask the congregation, and ask all the local traders who struggle with shoplifters.'

After some discussion, Father Janus and Dymphna agreed to give it another go. They asked the congregation for help, I went round all the local traders, and we all took part in the prayers. And the results? Well, they weren't miraculous. But we got enough. And we kept getting enough, week after week after week. I saw people being transformed again, former addicts becoming volunteers, and dying people coming back to life. The chapel community was buzzing.

Then the blow came, in the form of a letter from the religious authorities, ordering Deacon Dymphna to transfer to another chapel and congregation. I came into the office as Father Janus was discussing the order with her.

'Can't I just say no?' she said as I entered.

I saw their concerned faces and asked them, 'What's up?'

Father Janus passed me the letter. I read it and handed it back.

'I don't understand,' I said. 'What's caused this?'

'We've fallen behind in our payments to the religious authorities. They expect us to pay 700 rials a month towards Father Janus's stipend and a further 250 rials a month for me. We've only been managing about 500 rials, about half what we should.'

'I still don't understand. Surely the authorities should be paying you, not you the authorities.' Then an unpleasant thought crossed my mind. 'Has everything I've been doing caused you this problem?'

'No, Astell,' Father Janus said, his voice reassuring. 'If anything, you've helped improve our financial situation a little. More people attend the chapel regularly now you're looking after the building so well. It's just that we've not been able to pay our way ever since the authorities changed the rules. They used to base the payments on the size of the congregation. Now they base it on the number of households and the amount they think the area as a whole should be able to give.'

'Can't we just ask them to change the rules back again?'

The priest shook his head. 'Sadly, it doesn't work like that.'

Dymphna left us a month later. Before she left, she showed me how to look after the chapel's accounts, where I saw for myself the effects of the religious authorities' change in finance rules. Fortunately, two of our group volunteers took over much of my work in the day kitchen, which freed me to do more administration for Father Janus – not my best skill.

Twenty people from our chapel attended Dymphna's welcome service at her new posting, the temple in Roda. The temple was situated in a prosperous-looking suburb on the far side of the capital. Its fixtures, fittings, and décor looked new and were in good condition, and the worship hall chairs had comfortable cushioned seats. The temple staff included three priests and three deacons prior to Dymphna's arrival. I listened to the homily by the arch-priest about Dymphna's calling to the temple to work with the poor as scriptures required of us. His words rang hollowly in my ears. Dymphna had been taken from a chapel working in the heart of poverty to serve in a temple far richer than ours, just because we could not pay the authorities' greedy demands.

I felt called to change that somehow.

4:6

Fayell found instant favour at the mental health support centre in Chana. As with most care services in Ouslau, the centre was attached to a place of worship, a stupa of The Wheel. The practice of meditation was a core treatment for the people who needed the centre's support, and many found it therapeutic when they eventually managed to quieten their racing minds.

After a few weeks working at the centre, Fayell took over responsibility for the women's unit, promoted by Priest Dechen, who was in charge of the centre. She loved the work, helping the women in her care come to terms with their past issues and rise above them to start again.

Sometimes I would join one of Fayell's sessions when I had time off. She invited me there to tell my story of starting over to give hope to the women who heard me that a better life was possible in the future if they tried making small changes today.

Most of the women staying in the support centre had been victims of violence: domestic, criminal or both. They had very low self-esteem and their self-talk reflected the criticism inflicted on them by their abusers. I remember one woman in particular, who called herself Shadow. The first weeks after she arrived there, she sat hunched down on her chair as if she was trying to take up as little space as possible, and she never looked other people in the eye.

'I know the gang who tried to kill me are still out there, waiting,' I said in my share to the group. 'But The Shark's not going to stop me being the person I want to be. I refuse to live in fear for the rest of my life.'

Shadow's head jerked up about two degrees. 'But they're everywhere,' she whispered in a deep, smoky voice.

Fayell looked at me. It was the first time either of us had heard her speak in one of the sessions.

'I changed my playground. You can too,' I said.

'What's the point? I'm just no good.'

'Is that what they told you?' Fayell asked her.

She nodded, unable to speak further. Fayell put her arm round her shoulders and whispered words of comfort to her. Fayell called it *loving people better until they learn to love themselves*. I took over leading the session while she worked with her.

Fayell took Shadow under her wing and taught her how to change the narrative of her self-talk from denigration to affirmation. With Fayell's combination of group meetings, one-to-one support, faith rituals and meditation, she helped Shadow on the road to healing her memories and learning to love the child inside.

The next time I saw Shadow, about three months later, she had changed. Her posture was more upright, she looked at people's faces when they talked, and she spoke in the group session about coming to terms with her experiences.

'I used to think I was a waste of space, that the world would be better off without me,' she said. 'But now I know I'm here for a reason, even if I don't know what that reason is yet.'

The violence people like Shadow and other group members had faced and still feared prompted me to suggest that Fayell incorporated self-defence and fitness training into the centre's classes. Enough of the attendees were interested for Fayell to take the idea forward. Dechen seemed to support the idea whenever she raised it with him, but there always seemed to be some good reason why they could not begin: a busy calendar, reservations about violence, finding appropriate instructors. Somehow, those classes never happened.

After about a year, Priest Dechen invited Fayell to study for the priesthood. It was a great honour. After that, my friend was far too busy with work and studies for us to meet up often, and I missed our free-time chats in the National Garden of Worship.

About that time, Father Janus first introduced me to the Chapter Meetings: the local business meetings of the priests and administration workers, which helped the different places of worship work together rather than in conflict with one another. Priest Dechen also attended those, and when Fayell became a trainee priest, she came with him.

The Chapter Meetings were a revelation to me. I had expected them to be run like a typical committee, but I found the chapter had a rigid hierarchy where the likes of Fayell and me were not expected to speak, only to carry out instructions. That was apparent from the very first meeting.

The main item on the Chapter's agenda was property: surplus buildings, vandalism of empty premises and the high cost of repairs. The discussion went round in circles for some time. Then one of the older clerics addressed the meeting.

'We have a redundant place of worship in Wrosta that was looted by some homeless ruffians. Builders have quoted 800,000 rials to repair it, but we could not hope to get that back in return. What are we to do if we are not allowed to sell it?'

As repairing dilapidated buildings was very much in my experience, I stood up to speak.

'If you look at the quote, you can…'

Father Janus grabbed my arm and pulled me back into my seat, scowling at me. I looked at him, hurt and confused, not knowing what I had done wrong. He shook his head at me and then stood to address the meeting.

'Please accept my apologies for the way my enthusiastic support worker spoke out of turn. Astell has transformed our premises in Saunda. With your permission, I will arrange for her to help our venerable Priest Gazardiel repair his building in Wrosta.'

His undue deference to the Chairman was a side I had not seen in him before. It made my skin crawl. I sat in silent resentment through the rest of the meeting and observed the politics being played out there. The patriarch chairing the meeting exerted a condescending authority over us all, and the priests danced attendance on him as if their jobs depended on it.

I challenged Father Janus about it later.

'Why were you crawling to that elevated priest? The system he fronts gives us nothing and expects more than we can give in return.'

'I do it because they expect more than we can give,' he replied, his face resigned. 'They can close us with the stroke of a pen. Then all the people you help would have nowhere to go.'

'But that's prehistoric! Where is the humility all our scriptures tell us to live by? This is like some ancient medieval court.'

'Astell, you tell others to live life on life's terms. That's what we have to do here. We can't change the system. So let me do the pandering and you just stay silent.'

'Then what is the point of having Chapter Meetings? You might just as well send out letters of instruction.'

His chin dropped and his head tilted. He regarded me with hooded eyes. It was a gentle reprimand, but I felt it all the same.

At that time, Fayell was doing well in her studies, but then she began to struggle. A few months on, she sent me a note asking me to come to the session she was running the next afternoon. I had to ask Father Janus for permission to take the time off, which he happily gave, but with the warning not to make a habit of it.

I arrived early, hoping Fayell would explain the reason for her request. She was about to tell me when Priest Dechen turned up early, too.

'Just stay afterwards, if you can, please,' she said. Her eyes were glistening.

'Of course,' I agreed, my suspicions aroused.

The group session went well and most of the attendees benefited from coming. Fayell ran the group looking relaxed and confident until the discussion ended and we tidied up the meeting room afterwards.

'I'm just going to the kitchen,' she told me as she picked up a tray of drinking glasses, which needed to be washed. Her voice trembled.

When I looked at her, she mouthed, 'Five minutes.'

I nodded and turned away to help the others stack some chairs.

Five minutes later, I was about to enter the kitchen when I heard a man's voice.

'You want me to give you a good report, don't you?' It was Priest Dechen.

I opened the kitchen door an inch as quietly as I could, my hand ready to pull the knife I had always carried since my sailing days.

'No,' Fayell said.

'But I only want you to be nice to me.'

I threw back the door and leapt in. Dechen was standing by the table, his penis peeping out from his parted clothes.

In a flash, my knife was out of its sheath and impaled in the tabletop, only inches from his manhood.

His smug expression vanished, eclipsed by anger and fear.

'You could have killed me!' he shouted, hastily covering himself.

'Yes, I could,' I agreed. 'But I chose not to. Don't ever try that on again!'

He didn't. But he got his own back. When we reported the incident to the authorities, it was dismissed as being malicious. Fayell's first year assessment came round a short while after that. The examiner failed her.

His report called her devious.

So the lecher stayed in charge of the mental health support centre. Like keeping Herod in charge of kids' nurseries.

4:7

True to his word, Father Janus sent me to Wrosta to see if I could help old Priest Gazardiel with his redundant and damaged building. It was a small domed mosque with a crescent moon on the roof. The place had fallen out of use after its local worshippers had become more affluent and moved to a better suburb of Rabat. Then a crowd of homeless people had moved in, thoughtlessly damaging it through their carelessness or contempt, until part of the roof had collapsed.

The building stank of rotting rubbish and human waste. Even before I walked inside with Gazardiel, I knew it had been used as a doss-house and toilet for a long time.

'Is this still consecrated?' I asked.

'No. You are free to go wherever you wish. Just watch where you walk.'

The building must have been beautiful once. The walls had been covered with intricate mosaic patterns in colourful contrast with the arched white ceilings. Now, two-thirds of the mosaic tiles had been prised off to be sold as good luck amulets. The plaster walls were pockmarked and filthy. Part of the central dome had fallen in, and the floor beneath the rubble had caved downwards into the basement. It grieved my heart to see such a beautiful house of worship so badly treated.

Back outside, I asked Gazardiel, 'What would you like to happen to this building if you had all the money and people to do it?'

'But I don't,' he replied.

'That's not the question I asked. Let's dream a bit, let God onto the team.'

He laughed. 'You? You are asking me to remember God in all this? That is what I should be saying to you. Let's stroll away a few steps to clear our heads.'

He walked with me to a nearby play park. It was noisy with children playing barefoot in the hard-packed mud. I watched them and fought down my envy. My own childhood had never felt so carefree.

'If money and people were no object, I would like it to be a place of refreshment and hope, a place of prayer in action,' said the old priest. 'But how? It is falling down.'

'It is more damaged than Father Janus's chapel when I arrived in Saunda,' I admitted. 'But it isn't beyond repair. Let me see if I can find some volunteers to help you, people who have turned their lives around like me. Would you be happy for people like that to go to work here?'

'Of course. The worst you could do is make the rest fall down, and even that would be better than what we have now. What would you need?'

'Some of them may need a place to stay, and they'll all need feeding. We'll need shovels and rubbish bags, gloves, disinfectant, water, and something to take all the rubbish away. Later on, we will need scaffolding and materials. Would you be able to manage all that?'

'When people here see what you are doing, I'm sure they would rally round to help.'

'They may not see much at the start. Our first job will be to clean up the rubbish. Once we've done that, the smell should improve.'

'That, they will notice.' He smiled, a sad smile touched with a hint of hope and a glistening tear in his eyes. 'Thank you.'

Back at the chapel in Saunda, I asked the recovery centre users if any would like to volunteer to help me save the little mosque at Wrosta. Most of them knew what the place was like and said no. Just three young men came forward for the challenge, the hands of one of them still shaking from withdrawals. With Father Janus' permission, I left my deputies in charge of the recovery centre and went to work with the lads every day at the Wrosta mosque.

We laboured in two pairs, one shovelling and one holding open the rubbish bag, turn and turn about. After an hour or so, I stopped noticing the smell. I quickly realised how unfit I had become since leaving fishing behind. It was slow, filthy work, but it stopped us from thinking about anything other than the present moment.

Gazardiel came out to see us about midday. It was a relief to stop working to talk to him. We showed him the stacked rubbish bags waiting to be taken away.

'You are doing so well, all of you,' he said. 'Come across to my house for something to eat.'

'We're in no fit state,' I objected, waving at our dirty clothes and hands.

'We can eat in my garden,' he replied.

He led the way to his courtyard house nearby, adjacent to his temple. His centre garden was a serene place of benches and fruit trees gathered around a central fountain. A trestle table was laid out with bowls of water and towels, one for each of us. How lovely it was to wash and rinse the stench from my nostrils.

Platters of food had been placed on another table, nothing fancy but more than enough to fill us all. Gazardiel's wife served us herself, handing us plates of food and glasses of mint tea. The couple sat and ate and chatted with us. It was a beautiful thing to feel so respected.

It felt hard to return to work after such a peaceful break, but my companions set to with a will. We worked until sundown, when the light inside became too dim to see. Then Gazardiel took us back for a cooked evening meal and a place for the three volunteers to stay. I would have liked to stay too, but had to return to Saunda to help Father Janus with his accounts.

News soon spread about how well Gazardiel treated us. Our team of volunteers increased to ten. One was Jacob, an older man who had been a builder until an accident had crippled him. He had turned to opium to escape despair, but when addiction all but destroyed him, he turned up at our recovery centre and clawed his way back to life. With his skills and experience, our team repaired the damage to the floors and mended the hole in the dome. By the end of the rescue project, Jacob had gone back into the building business and employed some of the Wrosta volunteers as his workers. One was the young man whose hands had shaken in withdrawal on the first day and who was now relishing his new clean lifestyle.

The local school children helped us repair some of the more complete mosaics, using tiles taken from others. After we had whitewashed the ceilings, we skimmed the pockmarked walls with plaster and filled them with painted geometric patterns in keeping with the original building.

Some months later, we attended the grand opening. The unwanted little mosque had been repurposed as a creative arts centre and retreat hub. It felt a beautiful place to be again, and the local people who came to the opening pledged to keep it that way.

Gazardiel was so proud of our achievements that he told every other priest he knew. At the next chapter meeting, he told everyone there about the transformation of the little mosque and my part in it. The chairman was so impressed, he ordered me to renovate several other redundant and neglected properties. As I had no voice at the meeting, I could not object.

Once Father Janus and I were back at the Saunda recovery centre, I raised the predicament I now faced.

'It's one thing to recruit volunteers to rescue one little mosque for a kindly old priest and his lovely wife, Father. It's quite another to expect our volunteers to rescue every disused building in the chapter, for only bed and board. Greedy chancers!'

Janus smiled gently and let me vent my anger. He waited for me to run out of words before he replied with the voice of reason.

'Just give the appearance that you are carrying out the Chapter's instructions, Astell. Visit each place on the list they gave you, and write a report about the work needed to bring it back into use. When you give each priest a copy of their report, include a letter saying that no volunteers are available at present, but they are welcome to ask Jacob's Builders for a quote, as many of your former volunteers now work with him.'

His wise reply made me feel embarrassed at my outburst.

'I'm sorry, Father. Clearly, I still have a lot to learn.'

'As do we all,' he replied with that lopsided smile of his which this time seemed to console rather than reproach.

Over the next few months, as autumn turned to winter, I toured Rabat and its environs, inspecting derelict and redundant faith properties and writing reports. Father Janus helped me with the writing, as my schooling had been basic and I was also often too direct.

'Hopeless! Just finish the job and knock it down,' became 'It would make more sense to demolish what is left of the old building and draw up plans to rebuild.'

'Just get stuck in and give it a clean and tidy yourself!' became 'This building needs no significant remedial work and its few faults can easily be put right by someone with a practical turn of hand.'

One place, though, I really wanted to bring back from the dead. It was a buried holy spring attached to the ancient temple in Zenia, over a day's walk from Saunda. According to local stories, the spring had been about twenty feet below ground level, with steps leading down to a pool of water. All I could see there was a waste ground covered with rubble and some date palms nearby. Yet something about the place called to me.

As I told Father Janus: 'I'd never been there before, but it felt as if I had come home. This spring would have been dug out by our early ancestors as a gift to all future generations. It grieved me to see what had happened to the place.'

'Perhaps Zenia was your home in a past life,' he replied. 'Your fate may be tied up with it in ways we do not yet understand.'

'Does that mean you would let me work there? Even though I couldn't get back here each night to help you with everything?'

'It would be very good for you to restore the old holy spring in Zenia. Our superiors have noticed you've written several reports but done no practical work since you completed the mosque at Wrosta. Let them see you get your hands dirty again. Take some volunteers with you and stay there for as long as you need to get the job done.'

'But what about my duties here?'

'A member of our congregation has offered to take over your administrative tasks when you are away. So, go join the meeting tonight, and see if you can find some people to go with you.'

It took a couple of weeks for two people to volunteer from the recovery meetings: a young man called Nevio and a middle-aged woman, Ella. They had not known each other before they met at our centre, but got on very well. Ella mothered Nevio like her own child, having succumbed to addiction after losing a teenage son to sepsis. The young man appreciated her care, having come from a background of family neglect.

The priest at Zenia provided us with basic accommodation in a storage shed and subsistence food, mainly bread and occasional cheese. We picked fresh dates from the trees around the old holy well to eat with our meals. Our water came from a nearby public fountain in the central village square.

I made the mistake of complaining to my companions, 'It wasn't like this when we were working on the mosque at Wrosta. Priest Gazardiel really knew how to look after us.'

They just laughed at me for my resentment. As penniless recovering addicts, they were happy to have their physical needs met and something useful to occupy their thoughts and time.

We worked together in a relay, with one person filling buckets, one carrying filled buckets to the top and one emptying the rubbish into an old waggon and returning the buckets to the line. It was easy at first as we found the start of the stone staircase, but the deeper we got, the more steps we cleared, and the further we had to carry the buckets.

After about ten days, I asked for ropes and pulleys so that we could haul the buckets up and down rather than carry them. This was refused at first until the priest realised a derrick would be useful for people drawing water from the well once cleared. The next day, some poles, pulleys and rope appeared at the site. I put them together to make a working hoist. Our tasks became easier: one filled buckets, one emptied buckets, and one raised and lowered buckets instead of climbing up and down the steps.

We sang as we worked: mainly sea shanties from my fishing boat days. Their rhythm helped us dig and haul and walk from the hoist to the waggon and back. One day, the priest asked us to stop singing, as it was disrespectful. I looked at him, put my full bucket down at his feet, and walked away. He got the message: let us do this our way or finish the job yourself.

The ancient well we uncovered was a pool lined with granite flagstones, thirty steps down from ground level. At its head stood a shrine to the water goddess Ahanita, marked by her emblem of a twelve-petalled flower radiating from two central rings. The shrine stood in a niche carved into the rock. Two other niches had also been carved out, one on either side of the shrine. They may have held statues originally but were empty now and provided us with shelter from the midday sun. The peace amazed me. It felt solid, as if I could cut it with a knife and mould it into shape.

We worked on at the edge of the pool, taking handfuls of wet sand out of the water until our arms could reach no deeper. On our last day, the priest came and sat with us by the pool as the sun set out of sight beyond the staircase and the walls. After some time, he spoke.

'Thank you for helping us bring this holy well back to life. Long ago, an enemy army killed everyone living in this place. The soldiers razed the town to the ground and filled the well with the debris. Only the temple survived, because it had been dedicated to a deity the victors worshipped. We found it again by accident a few years ago, when we uncovered a wall while trying to dig a cistern. Some of the old writings say it is a healing spring. I hope it has been that for you.'

'I love this place so much, I don't ever want to leave,' said Nevio.

'Stay as long as you wish,' the priest replied. 'Take care of this holy well for us. Don't let us lose it again.'

Both volunteers stayed. I returned alone to Saunda, taking a flask of the healing spring water with me.

4:8

In my absence, Gazardiel had put my name forward for the regional Convocation of the religious authorities. He visited Father Janus and me to tell us the Convocation's decision.

'We discussed your membership at the last meeting, Astell. I said how everything you touch changes for the better: people, buildings; even my faith in God. They want you to become a member too.'

'No, please, no!' I cried. 'I'm not learned – just a sailor trapped in the city. I don't know how to play political games. I struggle even at the chapter meetings.'

'The reason I put your name forward, Astell, is because you are the only practical person I know who has the courage and faith to confront a room full of religious theorists. I want you to find the truth and to act as a mirror, to show them what they really look and sound like.'

'But why don't you do that?'

'I do. But I didn't have the vision and ability to transform the little ruined mosque at Wrosta – you did. I come from a similar background to them, so at best, the reflection in my mirror is very poor.'

I looked at Father Janus.

'Did you know about this?'

He nodded. 'You are not just a sailor, Astell. You are a quick learner. See how easily you turned your hands to looking after our accounts here at Saunda.'

'That's different. I had my own boat. Income and outgoings are the same, whether you have a boat or a chapel. I hate meetings. They waste so much time.'

'They needn't do. Go in there and see if you can change them, the way you've changed so much else.'

Gazardiel saw my dismay and stepped in to reassure me.

'You have the final say whether to accept the invitation, Astell. It is a great honour, not offered to many lay people. It has been made because of your ability to put things right and get things done. That's the talk of our Chapter.'

'But I'm not even allowed to speak at our Chapter. Will the Convocation allow me to speak there?'

'Yes. We will make sure you do.'

I gave in.

Two months later, I attended my first Convocation meeting. It proved to be three days of boredom. Clergy of different faiths discussed complicated issues of belief and practice, nitpicking about individual words when places of worship were struggling to pay the bills. Janus and Gazardiel sat on either side of me, explaining the procedures and helping me to fit in. I wanted to shout out, to protest at the waste of so much training and intelligence on things like the specific use of a single word in the doxology of a creed or when the first letter of God should be capitalised, things that meant nothing to the congregations upon whose shoulders the edifice of this talking shop was balanced.

Late in the afternoon of the third day, national and local accounts documents were handed out to all the clergy for study before the next meeting in three months' time. Janus let me look at his copy while the afternoon's discussions rambled on. Now, at last, I had something practical to look at.

The accounts documents were complicated: labyrinthine collections of pages which seemed designed that way to obscure the truth rather than clarify it. I worked through the Convocation's accounts first, as its budget was about a twelfth of the national budget. Even so, it took me over three weeks of my spare time to work out how the figures all related to each other, or didn't, as the case sometimes appeared. Then I followed the figures through onto the national accounts. The cross-accounts inconsistencies looked at first like incompetence, but the nature and beneficiaries in each instance were very similar and made me suspect false accounting.

I discussed the accounts with Father Janus. His eyes glazed when I showed him the figures. I realised he had number blindness. He had needed me to return each night from Wrosta to take care of the chapel's accounts because he could not do them himself. The volunteer who took them over had saved us both.

Sadly, before I could discuss the accounts with Gazardiel, the old priest suffered a serious stroke. I saw him three days before he died. He lay in his bed, no longer able to control his writhing body and unable to speak. All he had left was his hearing and a little strength to grip with his left hand.

'I found what you sent me to find,' I told him.

He squeezed my right hand.

'I won't let it rest,' I promised.

He squeezed my hand again. Tears stung my eyes.

'Thank you, for entrusting this to me.'

He squeezed my hand one last time. I am sure there were tears in his eyes, too. Not wanting to see the last of this old priest I owed so much to, I stayed there until his nurse told me to go.

'I will pray for you,' I promised him.

A whisper in my mind's ear replied, 'As I am praying for you.'

Gazardiel died two days before the next Convocation. The meeting stood for a minute's silent prayer for him before the proceedings began. The item I was interested in, the discussion of the accounts, filled the agenda on the second day, with the local accounts in the morning and the national accounts in the afternoon.

We were treated by the chief accountant to a fancy presentation of the local accounts projected onto a large screen. He whizzed through his figures with an enthusiasm not shared by most of his audience. I listened carefully, hoping his explanations would answer the questions I had. Sadly, they did not.

After he had finished his presentation, he invited questions from the floor. Most of the queries had already been answered in the presentation. I waited until the questions had dried up before I stood to raise my first one.

The Chairman ordered me to sit down, explaining, 'Astell Irva is not a member of the clergy.'

Father Janus stood up beside me. 'Pray let Astell Irva speak, if not on my behalf, then on the behalf of Priest Gazardiel who cannot now speak for himself and who asked Astell on his deathbed to speak for him. I would speak myself, but I do not have the business experience she has to raise these points clearly or understand the replies.'

His skilful diplomacy forced the Chairman to let me speak on Gazardiel's behalf.

'Thank you, Chairman, for letting me voice Gazardiel's concerns. Firstly, may I ask the chief accountant, what happened to the 3.6 million rials grant paid from the national accounts to support those places of worship in our region which are struggling with their finances?'

The chief accountant frowned, skipped through his slides looking for something, and then asked me to repeat the question again.

I repeated it and explained, 'You can see the 3.6 million being allocated to our region in the national accounts, but it does not appear in the accounts we are discussing now. All your income comes from parishes, property, bequests and sales.'

He pounced on the source of the money as an excuse to gain some time. 'We shall discuss the national accounts this afternoon. Please raise your question again then.'

'Thank you,' said the Chairman. 'If there are no further questions...'

'I have another question,' I interrupted.

A groan came from one side of the gathering as people had been hoping for an early lunch. Despite this, the Chairman let me speak again.

'Your accounts forecast a five-year accumulating deficit of 1 million rials per year. As this appears to be an operating deficit rather than a capital one, how do you intend to pay it off?'

Some of the gathered priests started snorting with impatience and shuffling their paper and their feet. The tense atmosphere seemed to shimmer around me.

'We will apply for central funding. The national accounts have 11 billion rials invested which they do so on behalf of the individual places of worship who had been granted bequests in perpetuity.'

'But we have already seen what happens in our accounts to money from the national accounts. It goes out of them, but doesn't turn up anywhere in the regional accounts. And another point: what interest rates are you borrowing this money at?'

'We will be raising the loans against our property portfolio, so it will depend on the contract at the time.'

'Let's say the interest rate is 5%. That is about the going rate.'

I took out a piece of paper. People groaned and several asked the Chairman to withdraw my permission to speak. That didn't stop me.

'The costs of borrowing one million rials over one year would be an extra 50,000 rials on top. If that was not paid, and another million was borrowed each year for another four years, the interest would compound on top of the rising debt. The amount due to be paid at the end of the fifth year would be in the region of 6 million rials. We would have to pay back an extra million rials on top. That is why the scriptures warn us not to borrow. So if this debt is being caused by operating costs, what are we doing to reduce the operating costs and the amount we have to borrow?'

Some of the priest gasped at hearing the true cost of such a debt. Others rose to their feet and tried to shout me down. As the Chairman quietened them, Priest Dechen leapt up.

'That's the woman who tried to knife me!' he cried out, pointing at me.

'Only cos you wanted a priestess-in-training to suck you off!' I retorted.

I had barely spoken when strong arms grabbed my shoulders and dragged me from my place onto the access steps. The two security guards frisked me, patting my body up and down with rough hands that went far too far between my legs. They found the knife strapped inside my left calf and showed it to the Chairman, waving it triumphantly as if it proved the accusation. He nodded. They dragged me out of the auditorium, almost dislocating my arms, and tossed me into the street. My knife followed, slithering across the dust beside me.

I rolled over to grab it, and looked up into a circle of camera lenses. The reporters outside couldn't believe their luck. They recorded every second of my humiliation. Embarrassed and defeated, I got to my feet, sheathed the knife and walked sheepishly away.

4:9

As I didn't want to lead the reporters straight to Father Janus's chapel, I walked to the National Garden of Worship where Fayell and I liked to meet. My thoughts were racing, and I hoped that the peace of the garden would calm that turmoil down.

Once again, I saw how my bluntness had caused the shame of being thrown out of the Convocation. But if I hadn't done that, I wouldn't have been true to myself.

'Oh God, help me! Show me the way through this,' I cried.

As I paused from my prayers, I noticed some people were walking up the steps to the marble portico of the temple with the cross. The three studded oak doors beyond the pillars were open for once. It was too good an opportunity to miss. I hurried across the garden to the temple and climbed the first four steps.

Half-way up, I stopped, ashamed of my well-worn dusty clothes, compared to the fine clothes of the other worshippers gathering there. I turned aside to brush the dirt off my shirt and trousers before climbing the last few steps to the door.

A smiling official greeted me in the doorway. He wore a black robe tied at the waist with a black cord and looked very clean.

I bowed my head in deference. 'Is it all right to come in? I don't have any money, so I can't pay.'

'Our services are free to attend. Take this service sheet and find a place to sit. We will be starting soon.'

I took the piece of paper and looked for a seat in the shadows at the back of the temple. Inside, the building overawed me: the smooth white marble, patterned by the sunlight beaming through the painted glass windows; the sheer scale of the structure, soaring up into the heights so far above. It had been built in the shape of a cross, with an ornate altar in the shortest arm. The congregation sat in the longest arm. A choir and some monks sat in seats blocking off the two wings, opposite each other across a beautiful patterned circle on the floor which marked the central crossing.

The congregation fell silent as a group of priests and acolytes processed in twos from a side room to the sanctuary around the altar. The congregation rose and the service began. To my surprise, it was exactly the same service as Father Janus led in the lowly chapel in Saunda. But what a difference! Where his was homely and familiar, this was formal and exalted. I sat transfixed by the soaring harmonies of the choir as they sang some ancient music by a man my sheet told me was Palestrina. I had never heard anything so beautiful before. It felt as if I had entered heaven.

The first reading was about an ancient prophet called Elijah who met God at Horeb. His cry really spoke to me: *I have been very zealous for the Lord God ... for the children of Israel have forsaken Your holy covenant ... I alone am left, and they seek to take my life.* The reading made me think back to a time when men had sought to take my life. Soon, today's newspapers would reach those men. They would know I had survived their assault and was very much alive. They might even know where I now lived. A pang of fear gripped my stomach.

The service ended and the seats emptied in front of me. I came out of the shadows and walked forward to the crossing to look at the beautiful tiled floor at the heart of the building. It showed a three-circled star inside a ring of twelve men, the black outlines etched into the amber tiles. A label nearby told me it was a replica of an original caustic-tile crossing floor in a cathedral in the old world, before The Destruction and the Treaty of the Alliance.

I stood in the centre of the star that marked the crossing, my arms raised in a cross, listening for the still small voice of God. It felt for a moment as if light engulfed me, turning me inside out. Before I could define it, the feeling had gone, and I woke up to the shuffling of feet and puzzled stares around me. I dropped my arms and hurried out before people tried to eject me from this place, too.

As I had feared, my face was on the front page of the newspapers. The first editions were just being put out on the stands I passed. I hurried back to Saunda, knowing what I needed to do next. Father Janus was waiting for me at the chapel when I arrived. With him was Fayell. She ran to hug me as I walked in through the door.

'Where have you been, Astell? We've been so worried,' she cried.

'I didn't want to lead the reporters here, so I went to pray in the National Garden. And I even got in to see the Temple of the Cross, the Cathedral.'

'Your ejection caused quite a debate,' said Father Janus. 'When they saw who had brought the charge against you, they realised they had over-reacted. They sent me out to fetch you back in, but by that time you had gone.'

'And go I must, now, too. My time here is done.'

'But your work here isn't, Astell. I'm sure we'll soon sort out the misunderstandings from today.'

'That's not the problem, Father Janus. It's my face on the front page of every newspaper, that is. It won't be long before some very evil men come knocking on your door to look for me. I must leave at once, before they arrive.'

'But it's been over two years. Surely they will have forgotten you and moved on to someone else.

'For the sake of your chapel, that's a risk I'm not willing to take.'

'Then I'm coming with you,' Fayell said.

'Don't put yourself at risk for me. They shoot first and ask questions later.'

'You put yourself at risk for me. How safe would I be with Priest Dechen once you're gone?'

Her objection convinced me. We agreed to meet at the little mosque in Wrosta that evening, and she left.

I packed my few things into a shoulder bag and said goodbye to my little cupboard of a bedroom. At least, I left with more than I had owned when I came there. As I went to walk out of the door for the last time, Father Janus pressed a cloth coin purse into my hand.

'It is small thanks for all you have done for us, Astell – just 20 rials – but it is all I have here.'

'I can't take that. Your need and the chapel's are much greater than mine.'

'For once, you are wrong. God speed.'

It was dark when I left Saunda. The streets seemed eerily deserted as I padded softly between the shadows, taking an indirect route to Wrosta to make any follower think I was heading somewhere else. No one challenged me on the way and very few people saw me. I reached the little mosque as people were leaving an evening meeting, and I ducked into the shadows so that they would not see me. But one person knew someone was there: the young priest who had supported Gazardiel during his last illness and had been promoted to priest in charge after his death.

He stood in the porch light with the confidence of youthful faith and called out, 'I know you are here. Come out and speak to me. Perhaps I can help you.'

I stepped into the light, unsure how he would react after the scene in the Convocation. He recognised my face at once and shook my hand.

'Astell. What brings you here? Surely Father Janus hasn't sent you packing after you questioned the accountant this afternoon? You said what many were thinking but did not have the courage to say. Including myself.'

'No. He wanted me to stay. But some very dangerous men will soon be on my trail, thanks to the evening papers, and I don't want them to harm his chapel. So let me return to the shadows, as I don't want them to harm you here, either.'

'Nonsense! If it is because of us you are now in danger, I have a duty to assist you. Come to my house with me.'

'I can't. I'm meeting a friend here tonight.'

'Then both of you come as soon as your friend arrives. You know where it is.'

I thanked him and hid in the shadows again while he walked back to his home by the temple. Fayell arrived soon after, apologising for being so long.

'Priest Dechen knew something was up. He challenged me about where I'd been and forced me to attend his evening service. I was only able to escape once the Survivors meeting began. The women covered for me. What now?'

'The priest here will put us up for the night. I'll show you the way.'

The priest did more for us than just find us a place to sleep. He gave us some nearly new clothes to replace our well-worn tunics and trousers, plus hattah headscarves, and his wife gave us a good meal: a rice dish with a spicy sauce, and fresh grapes and dates.

Next day, we set off for the holy well at Zenia. At that point, I did not know where I wanted us to end up. I just knew we had to keep moving and not to let anyone know where we were going. Most people ignored us on the road. On the odd occasion when someone tried to look us in the face, we drew our hattahs across our mouths and turned our heads aside in an accepted gesture of modesty.

We arrived at the holy well at sunset, just as Ella and Nevio, the volunteers I had left there, were shutting the gate for the night.

'Sorry, we're closed now. You'll have to come back tomorrow,' said middle-aged Ella in a bored voice, as if she had said it many times before.

'Do you not recognise me in my new clothes?' I asked.

She spun round, her face lit up with joy. 'Astell! What are you doing here? Is it true they threw you out of the Convocation for telling the truth?'

'Something like that. My friend and I are passing through. I wondered if we could stay here tonight.'

'Of course! Our house is quite small, but you will both be very welcome.'

Ella and Nevio shared their food with us and made up couches out of cushions on the floor for us to sleep. I slept well but briefly and got up at first light to visit the holy well. Fayell followed me there. We stood at the closed gate and looked down into the depths of the shrine.

'So you dug all this out with your bare hands?' she asked me.

'There were three of us. And we had buckets and shovels and a hoist. It's a very special place. Come and have a look.'

I clambered over the rickety new fence beside the gate and helped Fayell climb over it to join me. The fence wobbled dangerously, its support posts not driven deeply enough into the ground because of the rock lying only a few busa below the soil.

We glided down the steps to the pool and sat on the edge of the water, facing the three niches. There, we waited for the dawning sun to rise above the rock walls and light up Ahanita's shrine. The red-gold rays had just started to touch the carving of the twelve petal flower, when we heard a very loud bang. A bullet whistled past my ear and chipped a shard of rock off the lip of the paving near me.

We sprang up in fear and dashed into the shelter of the alcoves on either side of Ahanita's shrine. We could see the gunman silhouetted against the skyline, his rifle steadied against a fence post.

'Who are you?' Fayell shouted.

'Come up here and find out! You'll just make it quicker.'

'Don't risk it, Fayell! I know who he is – one of The Shark's henchmen.'

Just then, Nevio sprinted over towards the gunman, shouting, 'Don't lean on the fence! It's not safe!'

I leapt out of the alcove to shout, 'Get back, Nevio! Or he'll get you too.'

Another shot rang out. As it ricochetted off the stone tracery beside us, the fence gave way. The gunman and his weapon fell twenty feet, smashing onto the paving by the pool. The rifle came off the better of the two. Fayell picked up its pieces while I knelt beside the man's broken body. His back and limbs were bent at unnatural angles. He was still conscious, but in great pain.

'How did you find me?' I demanded.

'Car ... faster ... than foot,' he gasped. Then he grabbed hold of my arm, and I feared he would drag me with him into the holy pool. His face screwed up with all the evil inside him as he spat, 'Don't go home. All gone!'

He fell back after the effort. His body went into spasm and then went limp.

Nevio joined me beside the corpse. He saw the damage to the stonework, the blood on my face where a flying stone chip had grazed the skin, and nodded.

'Goddess Ahanita always looks after her own.'

4:10

The gunman's last comment prompted me to leave for Irva as soon as we could. The authorities at Zenia let us go when they saw how Fayell and I had been victims of an unprovoked attack and were not to blame for the gunman's death.

'Why are you going back to Irva, Astell?' Fayell demanded. 'This is what they want you to do. You're walking into their trap.'

'I want to know what's happened,' I replied. 'I left my mother, two brothers and a sister there. Are they safe?'

Fayell insisted on coming with me, even though she thought my course insane. She repeated that many times over the weeks we took to get there.

I wanted to tell her to shut up as inwardly I feared the same myself. Sad to say, the more she said it, the more my wilfulness drove me to go there. Without realising it, I was slipping from the golden way which had made me well.

We reached the port of Irva mid afternoon as the tide was coming in. It was a warm, cloudy day, with a humidity that made it difficult to breathe, even without the fear of what I might find. I went first to the house where I had been born, a fisherman's cottage facing the harbour. The house looked clean and cared for, with whitewashed walls and a glossy blue front door, but no one answered when I knocked.

We turned to watch the boats coming into the harbour with the day's catch, the seagulls wheeling about them as the crews gutted fish before being called away to guide their boats into their allocated berths on the quay. Fayell had not seen a sea-fishing community at work before and talked about every detail. Though I humoured her, I grew more and more downhearted. Our family's boat was not among them.

I turned back to look at my former home just as a mature fisherman was unlocking the front door to go in.

'Can you help me? I'm looking for my family,' I called out to him, hurrying over.

He looked me up and down, sneering at my travel-weary clothes. With a shake of his head, he said, 'They've gone,' and shut the door on me.

We asked the other fishing crews, but none of them would talk to us, not even the folk I had grown up with and sat beside at school.

I sat on a mooring bollard and struggled to hold back my tears. Fayell put her arm around my shoulders and hugged me.

'Let's find the chapel. Perhaps someone there can tell us what's happened,' she said.

I took up her suggestion, having nothing better to do. It seemed so inconceivable that the fixed world I remembered had changed so dramatically.

We climbed the hill to the little shul temple I had attended as a child. It had been a small domed building about the size of the chapel at Saunda, with a baked tile roof, whitewashed walls and a dark-blue door. Now, the doorway stood empty, the roof had caved in, and the whitewashed walls were grey with weathering. The ever-burning lamp and the benches had gone from inside. All that was left was the tiled floor, covered in rubble and roof tiles.

I sat on a stone outside the door and grieved for what had gone.

'We can rebuild this,' Fayell said.. 'You've done it before.'

'But what's the point? It's like this because they couldn't pay enough to keep a priest. Even if we did rescue it, the authorities would cripple us with more demands for payment and it would fall down again. They've left this port to die in its godlessness!'

I considered all I had discovered in the last two and a half years. A moment of clarity came over me.

'That must be what The Lore Keeper wanted me to see.'

'Then perhaps it's time to return to him,' Fayell said. 'But first, we need to find a place to stay tonight. This ruin doesn't look very safe.'

I took her to the Convent of the Sisters of Clemency, hoping that had not changed as tragically as the port. I shouldn't have worried. The convent looked its serene, whitewashed self, untouched by the passing of time. We rang the bell. A wimpled door keeper let us in and found us a room in the visitors' hostel. She invited us to attend Vespers before the evening meal.

We sat at the back of the chapel, listening to the ancient rite being sung by the nuns. Our bodies relaxed so deeply, we realised how tense we had been during our journey there. It felt like a moment in time which held all time within it.

After the service, a young novice came over and instructed us to see the Abbess once we had eaten. Fayell followed me up the familiar stairs to her office.

I recognised the Abbess at once from my previous stay there. Her face looked a little thinner, a little more deeply lined, but she had the same dark brown eyes, the same serene smile.

'Astell Irva, it is you!' she greeted. 'And who have you brought with you?'

'This is Fayell Orla. We have been friends since we met the Lore Keeper, when we both went to serve God in Rabat.'

'Fayell Orla, you are very welcome. How did you support God's work in Rabat?'

'I worked with abused women, and I also started training to be a priest, until Priest Dechen made improper demands of me.'

The Abbess studied her face briefly and nodded. 'I can see you did good work, Fayell. Try to forgive Priest Dechen. It is so easy to be contaminated by the ways of the world.'

Fayell blushed and lowered her eyes.

The Abbess turned to me. Her gaze seemed to pierce my soul. I dropped my gaze, all too aware of my recent wilfulness.

'You hardly need to tell me what you've been doing, Astell. We have saved all the letters we received about you, and even some newspaper reports. Here, look through our file.'

She passed me a slim red folder, its contents in date order, with a few labelled cuttings. The earlier letters came mainly from Father Janus and talked about my work with recovery groups. The later papers had been written by others: a letter from Gazardiel about the opening of the little mosque at Wrosta, a news cutting about the transformation of the holy well at Zenia, which did not mention me by name, and the front page news story about my ejection from the Convocation.

'Why have you collected all these?' I asked, humbled that the Sisters I admired so much should show such respect for me.

'By the grace of God, we have brought back many hospital patients from the brink of death over the years, but only you returned from Drysau Bridge. When you told us about your near-death experience, we knew you were destined to do something special. Challenging the authorities about their accounting was special indeed.'

Her eyes twinkled, as if she would like to have witnessed that scene.

But then her smile dropped, and she became more grave.

'Did you go to Irva before you came here?'

I nodded, tears pricking my eyes. 'What happened?' I asked. The words came out in a croak of a whisper.

'Your brother struggled to support your family with the fish he caught. He fell into the same temptation that almost killed you and took opiates to Sidion for The Shark's mob. Once your younger brother and sister had finished school and gone into household service in Rabat, he betrayed The Shark to the border police in exchange for immunity from prosecution.'

The Abbess opened the file of papers at a page near the back. The headlines read: *5 Border Police Dead in Sea Battle with Drug Cartel.*

'There was an ambush at sea and a lot of people died. It weakened The Shark's gang but did not destroy them. They worked out who had betrayed them and swore vengeance on your whole family. A few days later, your brother's boat exploded while out of the port, killing all the crew. With no other family nearby, we brought your mother here to keep her safe. The mobsters' contacts in Rabat have been trying to find your younger brother and sister. When your face became front-page news, one of them went for you as well.'

She turned the pages to the last cutting, which reported on the assassin's death at Zenia with the headline: *Gunman Dies in Fall at Holy Shrine.* I butted in before she spoke on.

'You said my mother was here. Can I go and see her? I need to say I'm sorry.'

'Yes, you can see her. But don't expect too much.'

The Abbess took us down to the hospital wing. My mother was being cared for in a twelve-bed ward housing elderly women. She sat in an armchair by her bed, fully clothed but untidy, as if she had no concern for her appearance. Her body swayed from side to side in time with the lullaby she was crooning to the knitted doll in her arms.

'Mama!' I cried, and crouched down in front of her.

She looked at me with vacant eyes and smiled in welcome.

'Are you the taxi? Have you come to take me home?'

My eyes glistened as I shook my head. 'No, Mama. I'm your daughter, Astell.'

'Astell died. Nasty men didn't like her. Kivvy died. Nasty men didn't like him.' She kissed the forehead of the knitted doll. 'I'm all alone. You're all I have left. Can I go home now?'

I fled from the ward, sobbing deep, heart-wrenching sobs I could not control. The Abbess took me back to her room to let me work through the shock in private.

'I'm sorry, Astell. I should have prepared you more.'

'Can she get better?'

'While we have seen miracles of recovery here, that is unlikely.'

'Then I must stay and take care of her.'

Fayell squeezed my hand. 'But she doesn't even recognise you, Astell. What can you do, that these Sisters of Clemency can't do so much better?'

'But it's my family duty.'

The Abbess contemplated us for a long minute before she said, 'You may both stay in our hostel for as long as you like, to give you as much time as you want with your mother, Astell.'

'But what about seeing the Lore Keeper again?' Fayell asked.

'That can wait for now,' said the Abbess.

So we stayed. About a month later, the Abbess called us back into her office.

'I have received a letter from the Lore Keeper,' she announced, handing us a sheet of paper. He had greeted the Abbess with the courtesy of an earlier era, and continued,

I believe you have recently been providing hospitality to two young women I had tasked with a quest some years ago: Astell Irva and Fayell Orla. If you are able, please ask them to return here with all speed and report their findings to me while there is still time for us to make use of that knowledge.

'What does he mean, while there is still time?' Fayell asked.

'The Lore Keeper is of a great age. He is experiencing the infirmities that attend that,' the Abbess replied.

'What about my mother? I can't just leave her,' I said.

The Abbess's knowing gaze told me how hollow my objection was, how wearying I found caring for my mother even with the support of the Sisters.

'We will continue to care for her until you return,' she promised. 'And I will arrange for you to travel with one of our local merchants to ensure you get there as requested, with all speed.'

'If you see it as that urgent, then clearly I must accept,' I said. A wave of relief flooded through me.

4:11

A week later, we returned to the temple at Sangha and were welcomed with great courtesy. We joined the communal evening meal after bathing and changing into fresh clothes they found for us.

The following morning, we met the Lore-Keeper again, back in the peace of his shadowy room.

He looked little different from the first time we met him: an old man seated among the books, his beard untrimmed, his hair wound out of sight in a turban. His great age showed only in his stooped posture and wrinkled skin.

'Welcome, my children. Be seated and take tea with me,' he said. His voice was not as firm as before and sounded more reedy.

We bowed and sat where he pointed, on the cushioned couches around his low carved-wood table. Once again, an attendant poured tea for us in dainty blue and white bowls. This time, I knew how to sup from my bowl, holding it between the thumb and middle finger of my right hand so that I could gently sip from it.

'Astell Irva and Fayell Orla, thank you for obeying my bidding and returning here from the Convent of the Sisters of Clemency,' he opened with a courteous nod to us. 'When you left here, I gave you a task to undertake. My correspondents have told me how you have got on, but that was from their own viewpoints. Pray, tell me what happened, as you understand it.'

'When we first met,' I began, 'you helped me see that though people worship in different ways, they all worship the same All Powerful God, whatever the name they use to call that God. What our faiths have in common is to love all, to care for the sick and the needy, to release captives from their prisons, including the prison of fear, and to turn our backs on wealth and greed.'

'But that's not what we saw in Rabat,' Fayell said. She described her experiences working with her groups of abused women, and her failed attempt to train as a priest.

When she finished, the Lore Keeper turned to me. 'I know of your work with addicts at Saunda, Astell, and how you helped save several faith buildings from dereliction. And I was impressed by the way you challenged the finance officer when you questioned his accounts at the Convocation. What conclusions have you drawn from all this?'

'First of all, the hypocrisy I saw appalled me. They preach that perfect love casts out all fear. But it is fear our leaders use to control everyone below them. Its poison runs through the heart of our government, from the lowliest parish priest to the ranks around the archpriest. That fear meant no one dared question the accounts or challenge the decisions of those above them.'

'Yes,' Fayell agreed. 'Priest Dechen used my fear of being rejected for priesthood as a way of controlling the projects I ran. He also used it to make me do things I didn't think were right.'

The Lore Keeper acknowledged Fayell's comment with a nod and asked me, 'Is there more?'

'Oh yes! I saw the wealth of the twelve temples in the National Garden of Worship. I wondered why our leaders could not also spare enough change to support the chapels, temples and mosques which serve ordinary people. Why do they bankrupt and close local places of worship for non-payment of dues, like the little chapel at Saunda where I grew up which is in ruins now? Our leaders claim to be people of faith, yet they are happy to leave villages and towns without a shepherd to halt their descent into faithlessness.'

The Lore Keeper smiled. 'Yours is a good question, Astell, and there is far more behind it than you may realise. Over sixty years ago, during the last world war, when Ouslau had but one national faith, the President ordered our Supreme Council to take over responsibility for all the money invested by individual places of worship. He gave four reasons for this emergency measure: war had caused the stock markets to crash, small investments were expensive to run, the Supreme Council's financial experts would deliver better returns than amateur individuals, and the size of the total capital investment would bring the best returns. There was a fifth reason. Our government was running out of money to defend ourselves and needed to borrow against the combined capital. He promised the emergency measure would be rescinded when the war ended, but of course, it wasn't. After the war, our land was inundated with refugees. Ouslau gave up half its lands to resettle them, and welcomed people of many other faiths into the land that was left. This caused dramatic changes to the way the theocracy of Ouslau ran, to ensure those voices were heard too.'

'So, if our leaders still get all the income from those investments to run our country,' I said, 'then why do they still need to borrow five million rials more?'

'That is another good question. Why do you think?'

I thought carefully before I replied.

'I think many of our leaders have become drunk with authority. They probably started out as people of love and faith, but temptation has lured them into sin. They have become addicted to the wealth and trappings of power.'

'That is a fair answer. But I suspect there is much more than that. As you can see, I can no longer go and find out for myself. Would you both be willing to go in my stead?'

'What about my mother?' I objected.

'She is safe in the care of people who are far better able to support her than you are. Your respect for family duty is commendable, Astell, but for now, let the Sisters of Clemency practise their calling, while you and Fayell help me in this.'

'I still don't understand,' I said, but in reality I did. Though I wanted to fulfil the duty of the fifth commandment to honour my father and mother, I also longed to escape watching my mother drown in dementia, and go adventuring once again. The dilemma still tore me when I finally said, 'It seems I must say yes.'

'What would you have us do?' Fayell asked, before I could change my mind.

The Lore Keeper rested his head on his gnarled hands and replied.

'I have heard rumours that the missing millions you seek are being spent in the desert. Something that costly must be of a significant size. Find out what it is and take photographs of it. Then come back here and tell me what you have found.'

'But that's like looking for a needle in a haystack,' Fayell objected. 'The desert is a quarter of a million square miles. It could take forever!'

'Set forth like Abraham into the wilderness, and trust your God to show you the way.'

4:12

We left about a week later, on a mission to collect the myths and folktales of the desert communities on behalf of the Lore Keeper. A young man called Andaf escorted us. He was the son of a nomadic family and understood the desert. The Lore Keeper insisted he went with us because of the patriarchal traditions of most of the desert families. Unaccompanied women turning up at a nomadic camp were likely to be made slaves and concubines.

As we were on an official mission, we were given camels to ride – an experience in itself. My years at sea enabled me to master this skill a lot faster than Fayell did. She struggled to hold on when her camel lunged forward to stand up or lie down and fell off several times before she got the hang of swaying with the rocking movement of the beast she rode.

We wore full-length sand-coloured thawb robes, black saya coats, and our hattah headscarves. I struggled to move well in the long robes after years of wearing tunics and trousers. The robes soon proved their worth in the desert conditions, airy enough for the baking hot days and keeping us warm on the cold nights. We usually travelled after first light into the morning, with a second shorter time in the early evening, before the sun set and night dropped like a stone.

Andaf guided us to our first destination, the semi-desert village of Eria. The villagers gave us a warm welcome as the Lore Keeper had written to warn the elders we were coming. I loved talking to the villagers and hearing their folk stories. Fayell took notes while we talked and wrote up what we heard.

When we journeyed on into the heart of the desert and recorded more family stories, we found that though many of the myths about ghouls, genies, and mythical monsters were common to most of the settlements we visited, others were unique to specific towns and tribes.

I remember sitting in a tent in Lahania, lit by just one oil lamp, with dark-haired tawny faces gathered round on the edge of the shadows as an elder retold one story more for the benefit of their children than for us.

'Do you know why we always cover our tents in dark canvas?' the old man asked them. His weathered face was like a mountain-scape of lines and creases in the poor light, making him look ancient.

I could tell the bigger children had heard the story before but knew not to answer, letting the younger children hear the story the way they had first.

The old storyteller continued, 'Our tribe used to have white canvas over our tents to reflect the sun. Our womenfolk decorated these covers with beautiful patterns made of triangles and squares. If you looked at them for too long, you could fall right through the heart of the pattern into the web of deceit.'

He looked round at the young faces, smiled and shook his head.

'One moonlit night, a sirrush flew by, heading north towards the mountains. Now, the sirrush is a huge serpent with leathery wings and keen, fiery eyes. Those eyes saw the patterns on the tent and were drawn to them. The sirrush flew too close for too long. Bewitched, it fell through the heart of the pattern and got caught in the web of deceit.'

He looked around at us all, making sure he engaged each child's eyes.

'The next night, the charrush flew by, heading north towards the mountains. Now the charrush is a huge jird rodent, with wings that beat like a drum and a voice like a throbbing roar. He was looking for his cousin the sirrush. As he flew over the patterned tent, he could hear the sirrush calling out from the web of deceit. He dropped out of the sky, tore through the tent with his claws, and released the sirrush from the grips of deceit. Then he ate all the people who lived in the tent. He flew off to the mountains in the north, leaving only their bones to whiten in the sun. And every time he saw another white tent with patterns on, he destroyed that too and ate all the people to avenge what one family had done to his cousin, the sirrush.

'So now, we only have black tents, so that the charrush cannot see us on moonlit nights and eat us too, to punish us for what our ancestors did to his cousin.'

The children's wide eyes gleamed with horror and awe in the feeble light of the little oil lamp. Even I had felt ripples of fear as I heard the tale.

Over the following days, we continued across the desert. Fayell filed the story of the charrush among the wealth of tales we had heard during our journey. But it still lurked in the back of my mind.

A few nights later, we were camping out as we often did in the shelter of a rocky outcrop, when we woke up to hear a distant throbbing roar in the western sky. Visions of flying rodents filled my mind. I pressed against the side of the outcrop, drawing my black sava coat around me to hide my body in the shadows. My heart pounded in my throat.

'Is it the charrush?' I hissed.

The roar came closer. The drum beat of the wings got louder and louder as it neared. Fayell moved forward to get a better look. I pulled her back into the shelter of the rock and glimpsed an oval shape in the skies with beaming bright white eyes.

And then it was right above us. The noise hurt my ears. I hardly dared breathe for fear the beast would see us. Then a choking smell of hot oil washed over us, reminding me of my boating days, and I realised what the charrush was. What an idiot I had been to let my fear and imagination run wild.

The machine circled round a quarter turn and headed off towards the north. We all breathed out as one when it turned its back on us. Once we were sure it had gone, we crept back out of the shadows.

'So that's your charrush: a helicopter,' Fayell said, laughing.

'But it's so big,' I said. 'The one the coastguards used was nothing like that size.'

'This one was a military helicopter, big enough to carry a lot of men and gear,' said Andaf.

'So the Lore Keeper was right,' Fayell said. 'God has given us the sign. We need to head north.'

That meant travelling through some of the harshest terrain in the desert. Andaf guided us across the inhospitable landscape: the salt-pan bed of a long-vanished lake and the arid rocky uplands that had once surrounded it; always heading towards the smudge of mountains on the horizon that shimmered in the heat haze and became invisible at night. After several days' journey, we left behind the unrelenting hues of yellow rock and sand for a region that was dotted with patches of prickly green drought-resistant plants I had not seen before. Our camels happily chewed on the plants, rolling them round in their mouths until they could swallow them, spines and all. Fayell and I watched the camels, amazed, while Andaf laughed at us.

Next day, he found signs that a nomadic family had crossed our path recently. He showed us the chewed plants and a little goat dung some beetles were burying for later.

'We are in luck. The Alfasadi clan is nearby. We should sleep in comfort tonight,' he said. He was right.

We were delighted when we found the nomads' camp of sand-coloured tents in a small oasis at the base of a curving rocky outcrop. They had pitched their tents in a circle under the palm trees. An ancient well provided them with water. Drawing it was always women's work.

The Alfasadis gave us a great welcome when we rode into their camp. Visitors were such a rarity that everyone hurried round to greet us. Children washed our feet, the men served us sweet coffee, and the women prepared a feast for us, roasting a kid and serving it with freshly baked flat bread and dates. The elders were pleased that we had come to record their traditional stories. They waited until the cool of the evening and after we had eaten to recount their family tales.

Once again, we heard the story of the sirrush and the charrush. Though the colours of the tents had changed, the basic elements had not. The purpose of the story dawned on me while I listened. The elders were quite aware that the charrush was a helicopter, not a mythical creature. They told their modern myth to warn their children not to be seen by the people flying overhead.

After the children had gone to bed, the men of the clan discussed the affairs of the world with Andaf. Fayell and I sat with the women in the next tent, but I could still hear parts of the men's talk in the background.

'Where does the charrush have its lair?' Andaf asked. I gasped to hear him betray our mission so needlessly, but couldn't do a thing about it without insulting our hosts by overriding their customs.

The elders also gasped in horror. They warned Andaf how foolhardy it would be to hunt the hunter. He explained that we only wanted to know where it was based, not to attack it. This hardly reassured them. It seems the Alfasadis had devised an elaborate system for never coming into contact with the desert interlopers in order to protect themselves. As they continued to warn Andaf off, a woman beside me asked me a direct question, forcing me to return my attention to the women's conversation.

The next morning, Andaf woke Fayell and me well before first light. He gave us goat herding clothes to change into – light breeches and knee-length tunics in rough tan cloth, with desert boots and brimmed hats. We set off soon after, travelling behind the Alfasadi goatherd up into the rocky heights above the oasis. He led us on over the pass into a wilderness of sparsely vegetated gorges, which looked like they gushed with water only once in a stormy blue moon. Our few needs we carried in panniers on our backs.

After a few days, the goatherd let us walk with him rather than behind, which made things easier. Though he gave me no cause to distrust him, I felt wary. I also began to question why we were following the goats.

One cloudy afternoon, we came over the brow of a hill and saw a valley spread before us, its barrenness split by a ribbon of new road.

'That should not be there,' said the goatherd. 'These were our best grazing lands, but now men shoot at us if we go near.'

Andaf worked out the distances and the direction of the road with experienced eyes. 'That is running from the border into the desert,' he said, frowning.

'We go now, before they see us,' the goatherd ordered.

We obeyed. But that night, as we bivouacked, Fayell and I agreed to explore the ribbon of new road the next day. Before Andaf and the goatherd were awake, we slipped away into the faint light heralding dawn and retraced our footsteps back to the brow of the hill with its view of the new road.

From there, we followed the course of the road, keeping to the rocky heights to keep ourselves hidden. We headed away from the border and went deeper into the desert to see where the road would take us. Now and then, we heard a falling stone rattle among the rocks behind us. We stopped and turned to see what might be there, but all would go quiet. We carried on.

Shortly after midday, we heard the rumble of a heavy truck crawling along the road, heading towards us from the border. We found a vantage point among the rocky outcrops and hid in the shadows to wait.

A huge lorry came into view, its fourteen-wheeled trailer filled by a massive rocket whose head rested on the roof of the cab. I had seen lorries before, but nothing even a quarter of the size of this dusty grey beast. It was to a standard lorry what the charrush had been to a sea patrol helicopter.

I opened my camera and waited until the lorry drew close. Then I took six photos: two of it coming towards us, two as it passed, and two as it went on along the road ahead.

Fayell and I waited a while before we walked on again. We still kept to the rough ground above the road, and we still kept hearing loose stones rattling down the rocks behind us. Were we being tracked by creatures with four legs or two? I kept my knife handy in case of a surprise attack.

Shortly before sunset, we found the lorry's destination. We topped a gap between two crags and saw a military base spread out across a plain below us. The base covered a large triangular area inside a long protective wall and fence which were patrolled by soldiers. Three separate groups of buildings with low roofs stood inside. I wondered if they hid a lot more underground than we could see on the surface. The largest building looked like a residential block. To the left of that stood a much smaller building which looked like some sort of command centre. The third group of buildings looked like a series of massive drain lids.

One of these lids stood open, ready to receive the rocket from the rear of the massive lorry we had seen earlier. We watched the rocket being moved into position by a mobile crane and the lorry's hoist. It locked into a mechanism sitting in the depths of the hole inside. I took several photos of the transfer and the layout of the base.

A commotion erupted at the gates to the base, and a helicopter took off. We turned to flee, struggling to scramble over the rocks and between the cliffs in the fading light. The noise must have drawn greater attention to us. We kept moving until we couldn't do so without risking a break or a fall. I crouched down, hid the camera between my legs to protect it, and curled up to make my body look like just another rock. Fayell wasn't so quick.

The helicopter came over the rocks, its searchlight combing the terrain, looking for us. A sudden burst of gunfire sprayed across us from above. Fayell screamed and fell. I turned to help her and got hit several times too. Savage pains stabbed my body as I fell back. I blacked out.

A wild dog woke me later when it tried to take a bite out of my hand. I waved it away. It shied off and joined the rest of the pack around Fayell. I wanted to chase the dogs from her too, but I couldn't move for the pain. Then the sun rose, and burned into me, and my head dropped back, unable to fight any more.

My soul rose out of my body and looked down on my mangled flesh and blood. I saw myself lying there in the dust and turned my back on that part of me. A path led through the rocky outcrops, calling me to follow. It led me away from the desert into some wooded mountains. A song beckoned me through the trees, and I walked behind it in perfect peace. But the song tricked me. I came to the edge of a ridge and found myself looking down on this valley of bones. Once again, I had to trudge across the skeletons of the lost, to meet the lost at the inn by Drysau Bridge.

MAGGIE SHAW

Part 5
Astell Irva : The Decision

5:1

I came to briefly under the beige awning of a tent, with faint memories of a rough journey in intense pain. Andaf's face loomed over me as darkness overcame my senses once again.

I next awoke in a small plain room, and found I was lying in a bed with clean white sheets,. A nurse sat on a chair beside me.

'Welcome back, Astell,' she greeted softly. 'You must have a fighting spirit. We nearly lost you several times.'

Memories flooded back. I recalled the inn at Drysau Bridge, the night spent hearing Daizin's and Ginny's life stories and telling them mine; how we had walked out into the dawn and faced the decision. Would we eat the berries and return to the lives we had wanted to escape forever, or would we walk into the sea and leave existence behind? They had walked towards the sea.

'Please don't go!' I pleaded with them. 'Please help me. I have to save our world from itself, but I can't do it alone!'

They paused and then turned.

'I am so tired,' Daizin said.

'What does the world owe us?' Ginny asked.

'I have no great words to persuade you. I can only promise it doesn't have to be this way.'

They shrugged and turned back towards the sea. I caught Ginny's arm to hold her back.

'Ginny, think of all those people you helped. Who will look after them, if you give up? Dulane? Kitty Derrer? Roul Khoury? Think of all the people who pinned their hopes on your police questionnaire bringing about real change? Who will make sure that real change happens if you're not there to push it through? You've got friends who can help you – Joe Kinder, Nahal Singh. Let them help you. Don't give up now, when everything you've been working for is about to happen but won't if you're not there.'

Ginny stopped, torn between her longing for peace and her sense of duty.

I ran on across to the beach. Daizin was standing on the sand, looking out across the sea of time. She looked at me and looked away again.

'Daizin, do you really want to disappear again? I know that at the moment, the choice you face seems to be death or pain. But the pain needn't last, while death is permanent. And there is a way back from this edge, a way to a place of contentment. All you need to do for now is to trust that there is a way, not just back to the pain you left, but through that pain, to that place of change and growth and peace you always wanted.'

She turned and looked back towards the ruined village and the ancient bridge.

I led the way to the bed of the stream and hoped she would follow. Below the bridge, a bramble was growing, covered with jagged thorns. A runner in the heart of the bramble bore three withered berries. I pushed my hand through the thorns and picked one. The thorns drew my blood as I pulled my fist back out.

The berry was about to touch my lips when two other hands reached into the bramble and plucked the other berries. We turned to face each other. Daizin and Ginny looked at me with drawn faces as they realised the implications of what they had done.

'See you on the other side,' I promised.

We swallowed at the same time. I tasted a brief bitter-sweet flavour. Then I awoke in a world of helpless agony.

A door opened. Someone entered the small plain room around me.

'Where are you, Astell Irva? You seem far away.'

It was the voice of the Lore Keeper. As I turned to look at him, pain clamped my body in rigid spasms. Defeated by my physical limitations, my head dropped back onto the bed.

'I've just come back from Drysau Bridge, again,' I whispered. My voice sounded like sand on parchment. Tears filled my eyes but would not fall, and I could not wipe them.

'It is a miracle you are here at all,' he replied.

The nurse gave him her chair to sit at my side and fetched another so that she could still watch me.

He continued, 'When you and Fayell slipped off to follow the road, Andaf followed you, keeping his distance to make sure that if you were ambushed, they wouldn't get him too. He saw the helicopter shoot you both and found your bodies. When your hand moved, he realised you were still alive and fetched the goatherd to help him bring you both back to the oasis. The Alfasadi used their traditional medicines to stabilise you. Then Andaf brought you back here to us at Sangha. Sadly, Fayell did not survive.'

Two tears escaped my lower eyelids and rolled down across my cheeks towards my ears. Inside, my mind screamed with grief that had no release. How could she have gone? Why hadn't it been me? And had our sacrifices achieved anything at all? Or had the evidence gone?

'Did they find the camera?' I whispered.

'Yes. We have the photos. We know where the base is, and we have the visual proof. You have done all I asked, and you have done very well. I am so sorry that in doing it, you lost your friend.'

He paused to pray for her and for me. Then he said, 'Now I need you to do something more for me. I need you to get better so that we can confront the President together.'

My concentration was fading. 'Don't understand,' I gasped. 'More than five million.'

He managed to unravel my scattered ramblings and replied, 'Yes, that base cost considerably more than five million rials. It cost five hundred temples and chapels, eight hundred priests, and debts in the accounts of every regional Convocation too. It cost the consciences of all the priests who govern Ouslau, and many their souls.'

As ill as I was, I heard the anger in his voice and knew I must obey him. I had to fight to get better.

My recovery was a slow process. It was made more bearable by the letters I receive from people I had known in Rabat and the weekly cards of blessing from the Sisters of Clemency. Over time, I left the infirmary and moved to the hostel in the temple grounds at Sangha. I shared in the communal meals again, with permission to eat at a table rather than cross-legged on the floor. My days were filled with exercises to get better, chatting with other people in the temple, and a few meetings with the Lore Keeper.

I loved sitting there in the quiet of the Lore Keeper's shadowy room. It had such a feeling of peace and timelessness. We sipped tea from delicate bowls while he talked about national and international politics. His understanding of these things went far beyond my own, but he seemed to appreciate me listening to his concerns.

Late one afternoon, he asked, 'Astell, how much do you remember about the two women you met at Drysau Bridge the last time you went there?'

I told him parts of their stories, in more detail than I had expected. He nodded in understanding when I finished.

'I want you to contact them.'

'But how? I don't have their addresses. I don't even know if they're alive,' I replied, thinking in terms of messengers and letters.

'They ate the berries. They will be alive,' he promised.

Next day, an administrator called Mell took me into the heart of the offices that ran the day-to-day functions of the temple complex and its extensive records. She showed me how to work their phone and the computer they had there, but she ended up doing everything herself when she realised how I struggled to use them.

We started by looking for Ginny Lee. Her profile as a politician and her constituency office in Paddingham made her an easier target to track down than Daizin.

'Even so, the cross-border protocols about data transfer mean we can't just look up her number and call her up,' Mell said. Her statement baffled me with its hints of whole worlds and sciences I knew nothing about.

'Is that where The Network comes in?' I asked.

'Oh, you've heard about that,' she said with a crooked smile. 'We will try that way, too. What message do you want to send?'

'The Lore Keeper told me to keep it simple. Say, Ginny Lee, please contact Astell Irva, and tell her how.'

We sent the message three ways. Mell sent my message to Ginny at Government House, Eleter, online using an international messaging service. I wrote Ginny a letter which Mell got translated, and we posted it to her constituency office at The Drop In Centre, Paddingham. Mell also passed my message on through a friend of a friend who had a contact in The Network.

Tracing Daizin was not as easy. She had used two different names, she had been based in two different regions, and she had lived under a repressive regime where contact with a foreign national might mean arrest, imprisonment or even death. In the end, we sent our message in four ways. I wrote two letters to Sister Sontell at the temple in Govensh, enclosing translations of my message, one addressed to Daizin and one to Yenner. We sent these separately through the official priestly mailbag. We also sent messages to Yenner through two different people in Aledion – Grandma Dora and Jael Losser – via that friend of a friend who had a contact in The Network.

We then waited for them to respond.

'What is The Network?' I asked the Lore Keeper, as we supped tea in his dim room late one afternoon.

'What do you think it is?' he asked.

'I'm not sure. It lurks in the shadows, trying to outwit governments. It has two faces, thwarting anarchy to protect profits through people like Roul Khoury in Sidion, yet saving victims and giving them new lives through people like Sister Sontell in Anoeth. But no one's ever mentioned The Network here in Ouslau.'

'The Network started as a response to the divisions created by the Treaty of The Alliance. It was created by people who wanted to fight the injustice of families being spit up, people who were forced to choose between communities and beliefs, and people who resisted authoritarianism. It first saw light in the temple at Govensh.'

He sighed and shook his head.

'Its nature changed in the different societies where it operated. In Govensh, it kept to its roots in the community of faith and still provides an alternative to those whose lives have been destroyed by repressive communism. In Eleter, where profit is king, it works through bribes and backhanders and street loyalty to support the little people trampled down by capitalism. And here in Ouslau, even though you had not heard of it, you have been doing its work, guided by people of faith like Gazardiel and Janus. Wherever those in need are helped to grow, the hand of God is at work. Wherever duplicity, death and destruction are sown, God has no part in it.'

5:2

The first call came two days later, from Ginny Lee. I had been hanging around the large office, trying to read a book, when Mell waved at me to come over, so excited she could barely speak. She passed me some headphones to put on as I sat beside her. I heard Ginny's real voice for the first time and could barely understand a word. Ginny spoke Sidionite like the native she was, while I knew only a few basic words from my drug-running days. Mell had to translate for me.

'Are you really real, Astell?' she asked me. 'I thought you were some sort of hallucination. Heaven knows, I've had a few of them, but that night at Drysau Bridge was in a different league entirely.'

'Yes, Ginny, I am real,' I replied. 'My companion, Andaf, found me after I was shot and took me to safety. I was hit four times and lost a lot of blood. It's been a long, hard struggle to get well again, but I am back in action now. How about you?'

'The healthtel staff rescued me from a snowdrift. They realised I wasn't psychotic, I just had a condition called hallucinogen persisting perception disorder – they call it HPPD. It kept giving me flashbacks when something super-stressful triggered it. They've given me meds to treat it now, and I'm a new person. What's more, Joe Kinder accused the Commercialists of trying to destroy me to cover up their misuse of power over our police abuse research project. He published the project findings on my behalf while I was still recovering in the healthtel. He's completely cleared my name and my political reputation.'

'That is great news. Have you heard from Daizin?'

'Not yet, but I have tracked her down. I sent a message to her Network contact, Grandma Dora. She sent a coded message back saying Yenner was being treated in a rehabilitation unit attached to the temple at Govensh. I guess, like you, she had been pretty badly smashed up in that road accident she had. Why, are you planning some sort of reunion?'

'Something even bigger than that. So we hope to contact you again once we've spoken to her.'

'Okay. Have to go. Recess is over, and I'm needed for a vote.'

A few days later, a phone call from the temple in Govensh came to Mell's desk. After various call transfers, I found myself talking to Daizin on a temple-to-temple call from Govensh.

'Greetings, Astell. I am Yenner,' she said in formal Ouslauv with barely a touch of accent.

'How are you, Yenner?' I replied, taking her lead. 'Ginny told me you've been very ill.'

'My rescuers said it was a miracle I survived. The medical staff kept me in a coma for several days while I fought the physical crises of injury and dependency. I am now being cared for in a rehabilitation centre in Govensh while I work through the mental issues that came with it. The story you told that night at Drysau Bridge inspired me to try again, but it is such a hard road, and I am so tired.'

'Always remember, Yenner: around the corner from discouragement lies success. Keep going. It will all be worthwhile.'

The call cut off. Mell gave a resigned sigh.

'Even our temple-to-temple calls suffer from Anoeth's political interference,' she said.

I returned to the Lore Keeper's serene chamber to report on our progress. We began work on the next stage of his plan.

5:3

Three weeks later, the Lore Keeper and his team of four travelled to Rabat to attend the National Assembly of Convocations. I went there with the team in a large black saloon car, which I found wonderful enough – so smooth, so quiet, so comfortable. Yet the Lore Keeper was driven there in even greater style, in a luxury limousine like the ones Fayell and I had watched crossing the National Garden of Worship when we had first arrived in the capital. I assumed the Lore Keeper had been given such a privilege because of his frailty, and I was only in his team to take care of him, which I did as best I could. His privilege included a luxury suite in the best hotel in Rabat. Through none of this did his manner change. He seemed to face wealth and privation with the same acceptance.

The following morning, we attended the first day of the National Assembly. It was then that I found out just how important the Lore Keeper really was in our country's hierarchy. Everyone who stood up to speak at the Assembly saluted him first before saying anything else. He sat there in his elevated box, serene in his embroidered white robe and orange turban, and responded to each greeting with a gracious nod. Embarrassed? I felt so ashamed that I hadn't realised his status before, I hardly heard anything of the debates that day.

I waited until the evening to apologise to him, in his hotel room after I had brewed his favourite tea and served it in the little blue and white bowl he loved.

He had taken great care as he sat down. His drawn face and his uncertain movements told me how tired he felt. Yet he smiled and invited me to sit and sup tea with him.

'I'm so sorry for not realising who you are, sir,' I said. 'I was so ignorant, I thought every temple had a lore keeper. You must have thought me very rude at times.'

He smiled gently. 'Astell, you have never been discourteous. You have always treated me with respect. There was no need for you to be aware of my true status. You would not have done anything differently if I had.'

He sighed and put down his delicate blue and white bowl on the little carved-wood table beside him.

'Thank you for your service today. Now go and rest. We have an important day ahead.'

I struggled to sleep that night for the boiling sea of my thoughts as I tried to work out how I had missed all the signs about him. The next day, I sat through the proceedings of the National Assembly half asleep. The speeches droned on in the background like a lullaby. An usher even had to nudge me awake once to stop my heavy breathing turning into a snore.

The President concluded his State of the Nation speech and stepped down from the rostrum. He had spoken in glowing terms of all that the Supreme Council had achieved. His fine words had borne little relation to what I had seen and experienced in Ouslau over the last few years.

Papers rustled as delegates tidied their folders, expecting the day's proceedings to finish at that point. The Lore Keeper nodded to the other woman in our delegation. She took the cover off a video camera and trained it on him. He then beckoned an usher over and spoke briefly to him. The usher conveyed his message to the President, now seated at his desk in the centre of the Supreme Council. On the President's command, the usher went to the rostrum.

'The Lore Keeper will now speak,' he announced.

Muted gasps swept across the Assembly. The delegates put their papers back down. A technician hurried across to give the Lore Keeper a microphone so that he could be heard without leaving his seat. The chamber fell silent. His quiet authority held us all in his thrall.

'Fellow believers in the Most High God, you who respect the sanctity of life in all its forms, and followers of the Faiths in their many manifestations, recall how privileged we are to serve our nation in such positions of high office. For most of us, that honour would be reward enough, but not for all.'

His eyes rested on each member of the Supreme Council in turn. I knew how telling that gaze could be, yet only two of the council gave any sign of unease.

'The temple at Sangha is honoured to be the repository of copies of all the most important documents relating to our country. This library is not just a storehouse. Our staff study and curate the papers entrusted to our care and use the information in them to publish our almanac each year.'

He paused to look down at some notes in front of him.

'To help us with our task, we are fortunate to use one of the few computers in our country. Computers are excellent for uncovering errors in accounts. Our analysts fed in all the accounts for the regional Convocations, and generated a report similar to the one our Supreme President lauded this morning. There are differences.'

A few more people were shifting uneasily in their seats and dropping their heads to avoid his gaze.

'I now call upon two of our analysts to explain what they found.'

The two young men in our delegation went down to the speaker's rostrum. I had seen them before in Mell's office but had not paid them much attention. One took over the controls for the presentation screen and projected a large graph on the wall behind the rostrum. The other stood in front of the graph and spoke, starting with the usual courtesies before he presented his work. By his fourth sentence, some delegates openly heckled him with cries of 'nonsense' and the like, but that did not stop his flow. He just raised his own voice to be heard above them.

'A key difference in the accounts we generated was in the allocation of income for different areas of ministry. This was masked in the Supreme Council's version by the way the accounts had been presented in percentages rather than amounts. We found that the total indebtedness of the Regional Convocations had increased despite their income generally matching their outgoings. We also found that about fifty million rials had been diverted from different sources to a project labelled *Pioneer Work*. When we looked for documentation to support this project, we found nothing of note — no accounts, no proposals, no description of its structure or purpose. We suspected fraud, but it proved to be far worse than that.'

By now, the heckling was so loud that the Lore Keeper instructed the speaker to sit back down. The protestations continued for several minutes. We sat in patient silence, waiting for the rowdiness to cease. When it did eventually stop, the Lore Keeper spoke.

'I had sent out a team of researchers to record the tribal legends and family myths of the desert nomads. One myth they recorded was about a charrush which killed anyone who saw it. Later, the researchers witnessed a military helicopter flying overhead and realised what the charrush was. They went to investigate.'

He nodded to me to go down to the rostrum and speak. My eyes must have been as wide as saucers with fear. The last time I had spoken in such a situation, security guards had thrown me out onto the street.

As I passed, he whispered, 'Remember Fayell, and tell us what you saw.'

I walked down to the rostrum. Rows and rows of people radiated out from me, well-dressed and impatient. My heart thumping, I handed my thoughts and actions over to the control of my Higher Power and spoke.

'I was one of the researchers who saw the helicopter. We were roaming with a goatherd and his flock: Andaf, Fayell and me. The herder took us to the borderlands. There we found a road coming out of Sidion into the Ouslauv desert. Fayell and I followed it. It took us to some sort of military base...'

Sounds of surprise and pointing fingers in the crowd made me turn to look at the wall behind me. A photo I had taken filled the screen. It showed the lorry, the missile, the perimeter fence and the capped storage holes. The image shot me back to the scene in a mental flashback: the heat, the dust, the fear and the pain as those bullets thudded into my body. I gripped the rostrum and shot an arrow prayer to my Higher Power for help. When my strength returned, I spoke on.

'Some sentries must have seen us. A helicopter flew over and fired shots at us. Fayell died. If Andaf hadn't found me, I would have died, too. It's a miracle I'm still alive and able to share this with you.'

A man in the Supreme Council fired a question at me, then another and, before I could finish answering, yet another. The rapid attack made me freeze. Prevented from being able to answer with the truth, I left the rostrum and went back to the Lore Keeper's side. People stood up, pointing and shouting. I couldn't tell if they were protesting about me or about the the Supreme Council and the base.

'Well done,' the Lore Keeper whispered to me. Then he turned up his microphone to address the Assembly.

'Pray, silence!' boomed out across the chamber.

People dropped back in their seats. Voices hushed.

The Lore Keeper returned to the measured tones he usually used.

'Since those photos were taken, my researchers have verified the position of the base. It is in Ouslauv territory, but the only road serving it runs from Sidion. We have seen the contract that was awarded for it to be built, among some papers sent to us by someone who did not agree to the project but could not prevent it. The contract for three separate missile bases was signed by members of the Supreme Council and by representatives of the Sidionite Government. The terms included bribes and backhanders veiled as additional services. Installing this first base cost Ouslau nine million rials. Our country is contracted to pay a further one and a half million rials per year for the next five years for Sidionite technicians to run this base alone.'

He paused to let us all understand the vastness of the sums involved. Then he continued.

'Ten missiles have already been installed. Their design and disposition indicate that they are aimed only at targets in Anoeth. Should Sidion fire those missiles, communist Anoeth's retaliatory missiles would target only theocratic Ouslau. Then capitalist Sidion would win the war and take over what is left of the world, and our ways of faith would be destroyed.'

He sighed and wiped his face. I felt the air change around us as the manner of the observers in the auditorium became more hostile. The faces of the Supreme Council members were like flint, so keen they were to hide what they were thinking.

'What the Supreme Council has done in the name of everyone in this country, is a betrayal of office, of trust,' said the Lore Keeper. 'It contravenes the Treaty of the Alliance, which bans the conspiring of two nations against a third. It contradicts the founding principles of our country to pursue only peace and faith and to respect the right of each nation to live as that nation chooses. It spent money that could ill be spared here, on a grandiose scheme which benefited only three rich industrialists in another nation and the four Supreme Council members they bribed to see the project through to completion. And it was dishonest; nothing of the project was discussed outside a select few from the Supreme Council to ensure that no one in this country would know and object, and none of its costs were transparent in the national accounts. Well, now our nation does know. Let our nation decide what should be done to undo this.'

He slumped back in his chair, spent. The President of the Supreme

Council stood up to rebut his allegations but found himself being heckled by the disillusioned observers in the auditorium. The administrative organiser of the National Assembly stepped in to call for a short break in the proceedings.

By this time, the Lore Keeper looked grey. I took him back to his hotel suite to rest, leaving the other team members to clear up after us.

Behind us, the Assembly dissolved into chaos, as the audience abandoned their seats and surged onto the stage, looking for answers and people to blame.

5:4

Our team made several copies of the video taken at the meeting. After adding subtitles translated by Daizin, they sent the videos through Mell's contacts in The Network to President Simon Falley in Sidion and President Lebistrom in Anoeth.

The media eruption forty-eight hours later told us that the two presidents had seen the videos. Lebistrom threatened to use Anoeth's stockpile of missiles to destroy Sidion and Ouslau. Simon Falley tried to distance the Sidionite Government from the deal: he claimed the missile base had been built in Ouslau without government authorisation, by a business consortium with no links to Sidionite military forces. It turned into a political confrontation even worse than the Freedom Marchers Massacre five years before.

Diplomats from our three countries got together and paved the way for a diplomatic mission to sort things. This time, Anoeth was the host, as it was the wronged party. Ginny Lee persuaded Simon Falley to include her in the delegation from Sidion. Our delegation from Ouslau included me, but not the Lore Keeper – he wasn't well enough to go. With the President and several of the Supreme Council under arrest, our delegation leader was the Ajari of the People of the Wheel, Tsomo Chodron.

The talks were stormy. I was glad our delegation leader came from a discipline which practised regular meditation and prayer. He brought a presence of calm to the talks whenever he was there. It was much needed, as Lebistrom was playing the victim card for his country, demanding compensation which Sidion refused to pay and Ouslau couldn't afford. The talks stalled in deadlock.

It was then that Ginny gave her speech, with Yenner translating her words into Anoether for Lebistrom to make sure the translation stayed true to the spirit of her words.

'Not long ago, I came back from the mythical valley of Drysau Bridge,' she began, causing the heads of the Ouslauv delegation to jerk up.

'I had wondered why, but now I know. This is a big moment in our shared history, the most important moment since our countries were first founded by The Treaty of the Alliance over sixty years ago. It's a time for us to reflect, to be humble and, most of all, to unite. What we do today, or fail to do, will shape the future of our nations and the safety of all our peoples.

'Ouslau, by hosting the Sidionite missile base in its territory, you've become the centre of this rising tension. Sidion, by building the missile base, you've not only alarmed your neighbours but also increased the risk of conflict. Anoeth, your demands for reparations, while understandable, are deepening divisions instead of healing them.

'Today, I ask you all to put aside these differences and realise that our ongoing security and prosperity depend on our collective well-being. Let's choose to accept that each of our government systems, whether democratic, autocratic, theocratic, commercialist or socialist, isn't inherently flawed. It's the human element in our leadership that causes mistakes and misjudgements.

'We've already agreed that the missile base contract was illegal and that the base itself is a threat to the peace and stability we all value. So, let's commit to banning all missiles from our three countries. This bold move will show our dedication to peace and mutual respect in the future.

'As we move forward, let's work together for the common good. Let our actions be guided by cooperation, understanding and shared responsibility. By doing this, we can build a future where our three nations thrive in harmony, where all our people live without fear, and where the wisdom and courage of our current leaders are reflected in the legacies we leave behind.'

Ginny's speech marked the turning point in the negotiations. By encouraging our leaders to think about themselves as heroes and architects of history, she gave the diplomats more leverage to create a resolution which would make all sides winners. Over the next ten days, the negotiators hammered out solutions to their differences. Ouslau's crippling contract with certain Sidionite industries was declared illegal under the Treaty of the Alliance and unenforceable in law. The three delegations then began to work towards greater international cooperation and future disarmament.

The breakthrough was hailed as a great success, with each side claiming that their country had been responsible for the new accord.

I didn't care who had done it. I was just glad a new agreement had been signed, and our three lands could live in peace once again.

The signing of the new accord gave Ginny, Daizin and me the time to meet up in person before two of us have to return home with our delegations. It felt right for us to meet here, in this beautiful temple at Govensh, the birthplace of The Network which has made such a difference to all our lives.

I'm so glad we've been able to meet in person, Ginny and Daizin. Thank you, Sister Sontell, for giving us the space and time to tell our stories. And thank you to the Big One above us, whatever you think that Higher Power might be – I'm so grateful today to be alive.

Part 6
Astell Irva: The Alternative Decision

6:1

I came to briefly under the beige awning of a tent, with faint memories of a rough journey in intense pain. Andaf's face loomed over me as darkness overcame my senses once again.

I next awoke in a small plain room and found I was lying in a bed with clean white sheets. A nurse sat on a chair beside me.

'Welcome back, Astell,' she greeted softly. 'You must have a fighting spirit. We nearly lost you several times.'

Memories flooded back. I recalled the inn at Drysau Bridge; the night spent hearing Daizin's and Ginny's life stories and telling them mine, how we had walked out into the dawn and faced the decision. Would we eat the berries and return to the lives we had wanted to escape forever, or would we walk into the sea and leave existence behind? They had walked towards the sea.

'Please don't go!' I pleaded with them. 'Please help me. I have to save our world from itself, but I can't do it alone!'

They paused and then turned.

'I am too tired,' Daizin said. 'The mountain I must scale if I go back is too much for me to face.'

'What does the world expect of us, anyway?' Ginny asked. 'I gave it all I got, and it rejected me. I owe it nothing!'

The two women turned away and walked on towards the sea. I tried to catch Ginny's arm to hold her back, but her flesh had no substance. My hand went straight through her and caught nothing. Daizin was the same.

They had already made their decision.

I watched them wade out into the water. The grateful way they moved showed how inviting the water felt to them. They released their bodies into its comforting embrace and were gone.

Life rarely ends in a defiant blaze of glory. It usually leaves with a tired whimper and a letting go.

It was so tempting to follow them. I struggled to resist and had to force myself to go back to the bed of the stream. Underneath the bridge grew a bramble, covered with jagged thorns. A runner in the heart of the bramble bore three withered berries. I pushed my hand through the thorns and picked one. The thorns drew my blood as I pulled my fist back out.

The berry looked old and uninviting. It tasted bittersweet on my tongue. I swallowed and awoke in a world of helpless agony.

A door opened. Someone entered the small plain room.

'Where are you, Astell Irva? You seem far away.'

It was the voice of the Lore Keeper. When I tried to look at him, pain clamped my body in rigid spasms. Defeated by my physical limitations, my head dropped back onto the bed.

'I've just come back from Drysau Bridge, again,' I whispered. My voice sounded like sand on parchment. Tears filled my eyes but would not fall, and I could not wipe them.

'It is a miracle you are here at all,' he replied.

The Lore Keeper took a personal interest in my recovery and ensured I had the best of everything available to help me get better. It was still a long and often painful struggle. My occasional visits to the peace of his dimly lit room made a welcome break from the rounds of treatment and exercise.

Late one afternoon, the Lore Keeper asked, 'Astell, how much do you remember about the two women you met at Drysau Bridge the last time you went there?'

I told him parts of their stories, recalling more detail than I had expected. He nodded in understanding when I finished.

'I want you to try to contact them.'

'But how? I don't have their addresses. I don't even know if they're alive,' I replied, thinking in terms of messengers and letters.

'Nevertheless, we must try,' he insisted.

Next day, an administrator called Mell took me into the heart of the offices that ran the day-to-day functions of the temple complex and its extensive records. She showed me how to use their phone and computer but ended up doing everything herself when she realised how I struggled to use such things.

We started by looking for Ginny Lee. Her profile as a politician and her constituency office in Paddingham made her an easier target to track down than Daizin. We sent a message asking her to contact me in three ways: through an international computer messaging service, by letter to her constituency office, and through a friend of a friend who had a contact in The Network.

Tracing Daizin Keberin was not as easy. We sent her messages through Priestess Sontell at the temple in Govensh using official priestly channels, and through Grandma Dora in Aledion via that friend of a friend who had a contact in The Network. We then had to wait for a response.

Our first response came two days later, from Ginny Lee's constituency office. They sent us electronic copies of two newspaper articles, which Mell had to translate for me. The first article described how Ginny had fallen into a snowdrift and died of exposure in the mountains above Cierte. The second article was her obituary.

I grieved for the vibrant young politician who had been destroyed by all the vested interests campaigning against her. Mell rested her hand on my shoulder in sympathy.

A few days after that, a letter arrived for us from Priestess Sontell in Govensh. It had been handwritten in Ouslauv. After the traditional temple greetings, the letter continued:

With great sadness, we have to report that the woman you enquired about, Yenner Devlin, died in a road accident in the mountains near her home in Aledion about four months ago, the day after her father died at their farm.

I grieved again for Daizin Keberin, the young woman who had done no wrong yet had been destroyed by the people and politics around her.

6:2

Three weeks later, I travelled with the Lore Keeper and his team to Rabat to attend the National Assembly of Convocations. It was there the Lore Keeper presented what Fayell and I had found in the deserts of Ouslau.

I stood at the rostrum. Rows and rows of people radiated out from me, well dressed and impatient. My heart was thumping – the last time I had spoken at a big meeting like this, the security guards had thrown me out. I handed my thoughts and fears over to the care of my Higher Power and began to speak.

'We found a road in the borderlands that ran from Sidion into the Ouslauv desert. It took us to some sort of military base…'

Sounds of surprise and pointing fingers in the crowd made me turn to look at the wall behind me. One of my photos was splashed across the screen, showing the lorry, the missile, the perimeter fence and the capped storage holes. The image shot me back to the scene in a mental flashback: the heat, the dust, the fear and the pain as those bullets thudded into my body. I gripped the rostrum and shot an arrow prayer to my Higher Power for help. When my strength returned, I spoke on.

'Some sentries fired shots at us. Fayell died. If Andaf hadn't found me, I would have died, too. It's a miracle I'm still alive and able to share this with you.'

A man in the Supreme Council fired a question at me, then another and, before I could finish answering, yet another. The rapid attack made me freeze. Prevented from being able to answer with the truth, I left the rostrum and went back to the Lore Keeper's side. People stood up, pointing and shouting. I couldn't tell if they were protesting about me or about the Supreme Council and the base.

'Well done,' he whispered to me. Then he turned up his microphone to address the Assembly.

'Pray, silence!' boomed out across the chamber.

People dropped back in their seats. Voices hushed.

The Lore Keeper returned to the measured tones he usually used and delivered his findings about the base, the contract and the finance for it, in a scathing attack aimed directly at the President and his four co-conspirators in the Supreme Council. As he spoke, the manner of the people in the auditorium became more hostile. The faces of the Supreme Council members were like flint, so keen they were to hide what they were thinking.

'What the Supreme Council has done in the name of everyone in this country, is a betrayal of office, of trust,' said the Lore Keeper. 'It contravenes the Treaty of the Alliance, which bans the conspiring of two nations against a third. It contradicts the founding principles of our country to pursue only peace and faith and to respect the right of each nation to live as that nation chooses. It spent money that could ill be spared here, on a grandiose scheme which benefited only three rich industrialists in another nation and the four Supreme Council members they bribed to see the project through to completion. And it was dishonest; nothing of the project was discussed outside a select few from the Supreme Council to ensure that no one in this country would know and object, and none of its costs were transparent in the national accounts. Well, now our nation does know. Let our nation decide what should be done to undo this.'

He slumped back in his chair, spent. The President of the Supreme Council stood up to rebut his allegations but found himself being heckled by the disillusioned observers in the auditorium. The administrative organiser of the National Assembly stepped in to call for a short break in the proceedings.

By this time, the Lore Keeper looked grey. I took him back to his hotel suite to rest, leaving the other team members to clear up after us.

Behind us, the Assembly dissolved into chaos, as the audience abandoned their seats and surged onto the stage, looking for answers and people to blame.

6:3

Next day, copies of the video we had taken at the meeting were flown to contacts in The Network in Sidion and Anoeth. Mell sent translations with them.

The media eruption two days later told us that those contacts had managed to get the videos in front of the two presidents.

Lebistrom held a press conference in response. He had clearly not used Mell's translation of the video, and his reported quotes from the transcript made claims of things I knew weren't there. If only Daizin had been alive to make a truer translation, I thought.

Cameras flashed and microphones crowded the lectern as Lebistrom announced, 'The Anoether people take the construction of the base to be an act of warfare. We give twenty-four hours' notice of our retaliation, if the Ouslauv stockpiles of missiles are not immediately destroyed.'

Political reporters confirmed Anoeth had a huge stockpile of missiles which could completely obliterate both Sidion and Ouslau.

In response, Simon Falley tried to absolve the Sidionite government at his press conference.

'The missile base in Ouslau was built without government authorisation by a business consortium with no links to Sidionite military forces,' he claimed. Even I knew that wasn't the reply needed when the future of our world was at stake. I wished Ginny had been alive to give a better speech, one that would have mended things instead of driving them further apart.

Then our own Supreme Council announced, 'The independent nation of Ouslau has as much right to possess missile technology as our neighbours Sidion and Anoeth. We arranged for the construction of the base to ensure our protection, not to become aggressors.' No apology. No admission of wrong, despite the revelations on the video we had sent, which all the politicians had seen.

Diplomats from all three countries tried to intervene, but Lebistrom was adamant. I watched the Anoether President's last defiant broadcast, as I sat by the Lore Keeper in his luxury hotel suite.

'So the world is to be destroyed by self-will run riot,' the Lore Keeper sighed.

We shared a last pot of tea, sipped from his fragile blue and white bowls. Then he told me to go, to make peace with my God as he had already made peace with his.

Sad that the Lore Keeper no longer wanted me, I walked away from Rabat into the evening, hoping I would reach Zenia before the first of the missiles struck. This place has always felt special to me, and I am proud of all we did here, Ella and Nevio.

You were already awake when I got here shortly before first light. I can see you have done such a good job of caring for this holy well since I left. Thank you for still being here and for listening to me.

Dawn is now breaking. It is good to sit by these serene waters with you both.

There goes the first of the missiles. May Ahanita grant us safe passage from this world into the next.

THE END

LIST OF CHARACTERS

Alfasadi	Nomadic tribe, The Great Desert, Ouslau
Andaf	Nomad and guide, Ouslau
Astell Irva	Sailor and recovery group worker, Ouslau
Benson	Ginny Lee's neighbour, Paddingham, Sidion
Corrin Alcheth	Security Guard, Anoeth
Daizin Keberin	Translator and labourer, Anoeth
Dawn Messenger	Neighbour of Ginny Lee's mother, Sidion
DCI Smith, DI Brown	Paddingham policemen, Sidion
Dee, Bee	Network agents in Eleter, Sidion
Demos	Innkeeper at Drysau Bridge
Duckie	Research student, Paddingham, Sidion
Dulane Ellis	Political fixer, Eleter, Sidion
Dymphna	Deacon at Saunda Chapel, Ouslau
EBC	Left-wing Eleter Broadcasting Co., Sidion
Ella	Volunteer at Zenia, Ouslau
Enn	Network courier, Sidion
Emmy Whitley	Daizin's birth mother, Anoeth
Ericsen Arayon	Paddingham Liberal candidate, Sidion
Esterin/Eston	Freedom worker, Daizin's lover, Anoeth
Estevan	The baby Daizin lost
Father Janus	Priest of Saunda Chapel, Ouslau
Fayell Orla	Astell's friend, women's groups leader, Ouslau
Gazardiel	Priest at Wrosta, Ouslau
Ginny Lee	Politician, Paddingham, Sidion
Grandma Dora	Matriarch of Aledion, Anoeth
Grandma	Ginny Lee's grandmother, Aldham, Sidion
Granthi	One of the leaders, Sangha Temple, Ouslau
Hannay	Farmhand, Sontey farm, Aledion, Anoeth
Jacob the Builder	Volunteer at Wrosta, Ouslau
Jael Losser	Innkeeper in Aledion, Anoeth
James Lee	Ginny's father, Deputy Head, National Bureau Ewlham, Sidion
Janie	Volunteer at The Drop In, Paddingham, Sidion

LIST OF CHARACTERS

Jazz	Replaced Dulane at The Drop In Centre, Sidion
Jean Swift	Director of The Training Bureau, Eleter, Sidion
Jemeth Whitley	Farmer, Daizin's birth father, Anoeth
Joe Kinder	Liberal Representative for Cierte, Sidion
Kaido	Drop In Centre volunteer, Paddingham, Sidion
Kitty Derrer	Network contact for The Drop In, Sidion
Kivvy	Astell's brother, fisherman, Irva, Ouslau
Lebistrom	President of communist Anoeth
Lois	Emmy Whitley's sister, Eleter, Sidion
Lore Keeper	Jathedar of Sangha Temple, Ouslau
Marcus	Ginny Lee's neighbour, Paddingham, Sidion
Mell	Administrator at Sangha Temple, Ouslau
Mother	Ginny Lee's mother, Eleter, Sidion
Mr Green	Ginny Lee's lawyer following kidnap, Sidion
Mr Sinclair	Psychiatrist, Eleter, Sidion
Nahal Singh	Shopkeeper, landlord, Paddingham, Sidion
Nevio	Volunteer at Zenia, Ouslau
Priest Dechen	Chana stupa priest, Ouslau
Rosheem	Motorbike courier, Aledion, Anoeth
Roul Khoury	Network leader, Eleter, Sidion
Salomon Marchon	Commercialist candidate for Paddingham, Sidion
Sam Derrer	Kitty's husband and hard man, Eleter, Sidion
Segan the Carpenter	Old lag in ex-cons hostel, Govensh, Anoeth
Shadow	Woman helped by Fayell and Astell, Ouslau
Simon Falley	President, Commercialist Leader, Sidion
Sister Mercy	Convent of the Sisters of Clemency, Ouslau
Sister Patience	Convent of the Sisters of Clemency, Ouslau
Sister Sontell	Priest at Govensh Temple, Anoeth
Smoky Jim's Bar	Bar, drug den, Paddingham, Sidion
Stacey Foster	Lawyers for All lawyer, Eleter, Sidion
The Shark	Drug cartel boss at Irva, Ouslau
Tsomo Chodron	Ajari leader, Ouslau
Yenner Whitley	Daizin's new identity, Aledion, Anoeth

Thank you for buying this book. If you have enjoyed this novel, please leave a review at the online bookstore where you made your purchase or on our website, www.eregendal.com using the QR code below.
We read and appreciate every one.

About the Author

Author Maggie Shaw creates her stories from her many and varied life experiences. A teenage runaway who made good before her recent autistic spectrum disorder diagnosis, Maggie writes as one who has walked the walk in recovery and spiritual development. Her degrees in science, divinity and church music, and her career as a Mental Health Dietitian, give a solid framework to the exciting adventure stories she loves to tell. The Scottish hills and Lakeland fells where her forebears farmed often feature as landscapes in her work.

Maggie is also a church musician, composer and songwriter, and the stories she writes inspire many of her songs.

This is the thirteenth book Maggie has published through micropublisher Eregendal. Her music and short stories have been broadcast by Radio Carlisle, Cat Radio, and Red Shift Radio; and she has contributed articles to The St Raphael's Guild *Chrism*, The Church of England Newspaper, and *Soul and Spirit* Magazine. Online, Maggie also publishes through ArtSwarm, YouTube, SoundCloud, Facebook and the Eregendal website www.eregendal.com.

Maggie lives in Cheshire with her husband Alan and their cat, Tarby.